We Will Plant Birds of Paradise

GENEVIEVE RHEAMS

RATTLING GOOD YARNS
PRESS

Rattling Good Yarns Press
33490 Date Palm Drive 3065
Cathedral City CA 92235
USA
www.rattlinggoodyarns.com

Cover Design: Rattling Good Yarns Press

Library of Congress Control Number: 2025940252
ISBN: 978-1-955826-90-7

First Edition

To my birds of paradise - Melanie, Claire, Emma, and Christopher.

*Love is the flower of life, and blossoms
unexpectedly and without law, and must be
plucked where it is found, and enjoyed for the
brief hour of its duration.*

~ D. H. Lawrence

Part One
1995

1

Jess was glad that her grandma Doris was sleeping. She hadn't figured out what to say yet, and she'd spent most of the last five days standing next to her grandmother's hospice bed in the room with too many rosaries. Her grandparents had collected one from every city their RV took them to before her grandfather died. Multi-colored beads bound together with silver crosses of tiny Jesuses hung from every wall, lay spread along the dresser and coiled in piles on the bedside table. Even the calendar on the wall was Christ-themed. Every month of 1995 had featured a different drawing of Jesus doing things like teaching and carrying lambs, but every month had the same picture of a rosary on the bottom right-hand corner.

Doris had been a nun until she'd left the Convent at the age of forty and married Jess's grandfather. The rosaries, she'd said, were a bridge from her life in the church to her life with her husband, so she didn't forget where she came from. Doris had once been tall, broad-shouldered, and pear-shaped. Cancer had shriveled her into dehydrated fruit. She breathed open-mouthed and deliberate. Jess ran her thumb over Grandma's clawed fingers.

"I know you," Grandma said, squinting.

"Do you?" Jess asked.

Grandma took a breath. "Louanne."

A pain hit Jess; she hadn't expected her not to know. Jess was fifteen with a long, dark braid down her back, running shorts, and a sleeveless jersey from the track meet she'd had that morning. It bothered Jess that Grandma had mistaken her for her daughter, who was twenty-five years older and had electric blue hair and a nose stud.

"Jess," her mother hissed from the doorway. She waved Jess to her. "Louanne called. I told her not to come, but she's not listening."

"Grandma was just asking for her."

"Lord."

"I mean, she was sort of asking. She thinks I'm her."

"Maybe that's a good thing. If you pretend to be her, Grandma can say her goodbyes, and we can keep Lou and That Woman out."

That Woman was Vivienne, Aunt Lou's live-in girlfriend. Grandma and Grandpa had refused to call her anything except Aunt Lou's roommate, which, to Jess, seemed harsher than That Woman—at least her mother's contempt recognized the true nature of their relationship.

"Louanne's caused enough heartache," her mom said. "I want my mother to have peace."

"She's Aunt Lou's mother too. You're not going to let her say goodbye?"

"She's going to want to bring That Woman. The hospice nurse is coming. I need to keep Grandma comfortable. We don't need anything upsetting her right now."

"Did she say that she was bringing Vivienne?" Jess asked.

"She's always trying to bring her around. I need you to go out to the driveway. Stall your aunt a while."

"You think I can stop her from coming in if she wants to?"

When Jess turned five, her mom had told Aunt Lou that she couldn't come to the birthday party. Jess had cried and begged for her to come. She even called Aunt Lou and told her to come anyway, but her mom snatched the phone and swatted Jess for it. The guests were all in the backyard on the day of the party. Jess was standing by a fold-out table covered in brightly wrapped presents and a cake with Sesame Street characters on it. Her school friends and family were singing the last few words of "Happy Birthday," and she was taking a gulp of air to blow out her candles when Aunt Lou drove her motorcycle into the yard.

Jess wasn't wild about the idea of standing between Aunt Lou and the front door. She drove a truck now.

"Tell her to come tomorrow." Mom ran a hand through her hair. "Maybe she'll listen to you."

"But tomorrow might be too late."

Jess looked back at Grandma. She'd closed her eyes. Her face had the worn look of the silver saviors on the wall.

"Just hold her off long enough to let me talk to the nurse."

She pressed a hand against Jess's shoulder, shoving her towards the hallway.

A woman in light blue scrubs was at the door when she opened it. She gave Jess a sympathetic smile and stepped past her. Jess walked out to the cloudless heat of the afternoon. She wanted to know what that nurse was going to tell her mom. She wanted to ask Grandma if she was really Catholic or if she just liked rosaries. She wanted to know why she and Mom ignored Aunt Lou for so long.

Jess crouched in the driveway. A doodlebug crawled in the space between the cement and the grass. When Jess was little, she and Grandma used to look for them in the yard. She showed Jess how they rolled into a ball if you touched them, but then if you held still, they would uncurl. Their tiny legs would tickle across Jess's hand.

Jess was reaching out to the doodlebug when a white pickup truck entered the driveway. Its brakes squealed as it crunched to a halt. Aunt Lou took her time cleaning off her sunglasses in the cab before she looked over at Jess and smiled. She set her shades on the dashboard and stepped out of the truck. Louanne wore a black button-down shirt, jeans, and black boots that clomped as she walked. She held a bottle of Dos Equis by the neck with her fingertips. There were deep crow's feet around her brown eyes and burn marks on her hands from handling hot bread at the bakery. Her pixie cut blazed blue.

She reached into her shirt pocket and took out a pack of Camels.

The inside of her truck had smelled like cigarettes when she picked Jess up from school one day. She'd blared a Blondie cassette and given Jess sips of her daiquiri.

"You keep it down here," she'd said, tucking the Styrofoam cup between her ankle and the driver's side door. "So the cops don't see."

Aunt Lou took a drag from her smoke. "You planning to go for a run?"

"I had a track meet today."

"Did you win?"

"No."

Aunt Lou held the cigarette out to her. Jess took a drag and passed it back.

"Is Vivienne coming?" Jess asked.

Aunt Lou shook her head. "I'd just as soon throw her to a barracuda. How is your grandma?"

"She's not good."

"She awake?"

"Off and on. She's in the rosary room."

"Jesus Christ," she said.

"She thought I was you."

Aunt Lou pinched Jess's chin. "The apple don't fall far. Your mom doesn't want me in there, does she?"

"No."

"Don't really want to go in, to tell you the truth."

"Grandma doesn't have long."

"I know."

"She wants to talk to you."

Aunt Lou took a swig of beer.

"Can I have one?" Jess asked.

"Help yourself."

On the weekends, Aunt Lou liked to keep long necks in a red cooler on the passenger seat. That morning, there was a clear plastic bag of golden-brown flatbread on top of the cooler. Olive oil glistened through the plastic. Jess set it aside and fished a bottle from the ice. Aunt Lou came over to pop it open with the thing on her keychain.

"What did you bring?" Jess asked, pointing to the loaf.

"Focaccia."

Jess took a sip of cold beer. "Grandma can't eat it."

"We can."

"Let's go in," Jess said.

Aunt Lou grinned. "You gonna roll in with a beer and a smoke? Let's sit a minute."

She went over to the back of the truck and pulled the tailgate down.

Jess looked back at the house. "We should go in soon."

"Who's all in there?"

"Just Mom and the hospice nurse."

"Come sit, kid. Let the nurse talk to your mom."

Why wasn't she trying to fight past Jess? Why wasn't she getting into the truck and plowing into the front door?

Jess planted her butt down so hard the truck shook.

"What's the matter with you?" Aunt Lou asked.

"Are you serious?"

She lowered her eyes. "She *wants* to talk to me, huh?"

"When she thought I was you, she seemed happy about it."

"Maybe you're a better me."

"Why don't y'all get along? You, Mom, and Grandma?"

"I'm a bad Catholic."

"*I'm* a bad Catholic. Are they going to stop talking to me?"

"Not unless you get a girlfriend."

Jess had thought that might be it, she just hadn't wanted to think about it. Her mom had told her dad several times over the years that she worried about Jess spending too much time with a dyke. That was how she'd said it.

Jess sometimes wondered about herself. She counted the evidence. One — she felt more comfortable around Aunt Lou and Vivienne than with her mother and father. Lou and Vivienne were gentler with each other; they laughed. Her mom and dad talked but didn't laugh.

Two — Jess noticed girls at school. But that wasn't because of Aunt Lou. Louanne had never pointed out a woman and catcalled her or something gross like Jess's uncles had. Aunt Lou never asked Jess about who she liked at all. Still, Jess paid more attention to other girls. She cared what they thought. She loved, in particular, watching other girls brush their hair in the bathroom mirror—intent on their lovely, reflected faces, focusing hard on the straightening of long hair, as if each brush stroke brought them closer to beauty.

Jess would notice and then look back at herself in the mirror. Was this what a gay person looked like?

Three, she remembered what her dad had told her mom the last time it was brought up. Her dad had told her mom not to worry. Jess had become much more feminine than Louanne. Feminine women didn't like other women, he said. So maybe what she felt wasn't attraction — maybe what all the facts added up to was just that Jess admired another girl's beauty.

"I was just hoping it was something different," Jess said to Louanne. "Like a fight y'all never told me about or something."

"No. I was supposed to turn out like your mother."

"I'm glad you didn't. I don't know if I'm really Catholic."

"No Catholics know if they're really Catholic. Except your grandma."

"Where do you think she'll go when she dies?"

Aunt Lou took a last drag from her cigarette and threw it into the street.

"I don't know, but I can't imagine your grandmother's spirit going nowhere."

"Me neither. Let's go back in."

"Relax. Finish your beer."

Jess tipped the bottle to her mouth and gulped it down, even as the cold stung her throat. When the last of the foam hit her lips, she set the bottle down.

"Damn, kid."

"Please," Jess said.

"Take a minute, I'm telling you."

Jess scooched off the tailgate and walked back into the house. The door to the rosary room was closed. Mom answered when Jess knocked and frowned at her.

"How's Grandma?" Jess asked, looking past Mom at the nurse standing next to the bed, writing something down.

Grandma was sitting up, talking to her.

"She's the same. Is Lou out there?"

"Yeah. Grandma doesn't look the same. She's awake. Is that good?"

"Go back out until the nurse is done."

"I don't want to. I want to be with Grandma."

She sniffed at Jess. "Why do you smell like beer?"

"Because I had one."

Mom squeezed her eyes shut and sighed. "I don't have time for this right now. I'll let you know when you can come back in."

"What did the nurse say?"

"Her heart and lungs are failing," Mom snapped.

"But she looks better."

"She's not. She might have a couple of days."

She closed the door.

Jess went back outside and sat next to Aunt Lou. Lou had lit up another cigarette. The way she drew on it so casually, so calm, infuriated Jess.

"You all right?" Aunt Lou asked.

"Why are you here?" Jess said. "If you don't want to go in, what did you come here for?"

"To see my favorite niece."

"Bullshit."

"I'm not bullshitting you. How long have you been in that room?"

"A couple of hours."

"How long yesterday?"

Jess searched through the fog of her brain.

"You losing track of the days?" Aunt Lou asked.

Aunt Lou laid down her empty bottle in the bed of the truck and got up to fetch two cold ones from the cooler and the bag of bread. She handed Jess the beers, sat down, and unwrapped the focaccia. She laid the plastic down between them and set the bread on top of it.

"Figured you hadn't had lunch," she told Jess, taking a beer from her hand. She clinked her bottle against Jess's in a silent toast.

Aunt Lou tore off a chunk of bread and handed it to Jess. "When your grandpa died, I couldn't tell you what day it was. Your mom had just had that hysterectomy. It bothered her that she couldn't be there. I was glad for the time. It was the first time your Grandma and Grandpa had talked to me in years. Anyway, I think that's why it means so much to your mom to be by your grandma now because she couldn't be there for our dad."

"The nurse told Mom Grandma's heart and lungs are failing. But she's sitting up and talking."

Aunt Lou's face turned grim. "They do that. They rally a couple of days before they die. It'll be a good day to see her, then." She nudged the bread in Jess's hand with her beer. "Eat that."

Jess looked at it. Hot tears filled her eyes and, she took a quick sip of beer.

"Come on, now," Aunt Lou said. "You should eat something."

"I don't want to eat. I want to be with Grandma."

"Eat that, and I'll go in with you."

Jess took a bite. It wasn't warm, but it was rich with olive oil and garlic. It was good with the beer. She and Aunt Lou ate quietly as they tore hunks of bread and washed it down until their bottles were empty.

Aunt Lou set the bottle behind her and wiped her hands on her jeans.

"All right," she said. "Let's go."

Jess followed her into the house. Her mom, grandma, and the nurse were all talking at the same time. She couldn't understand what any of them were saying behind the door.

"Rebecca," Aunt Lou called, rapping her knuckles on the door. She tried to turn the knob, but it was locked. "Fuck's sake," she muttered.

Mom and the nurse stopped talking. Grandma continued to babble. The door opened a bit, and mom poked her head out.

"Not now," she said to Aunt Lou.

"What the fuck have you got the door locked for?"

"You."

"Jess wants to see Mom."

"She can see her in a minute."

"The kid was crying outside, Rebecca, let her come in."

"Louanne," Grandma called.

Mom stepped out the door and shut it behind her. Aunt Lou towered above her.

"I told you to come later," she said to Aunt Lou.

"Mom's asking for me."

Rebecca turned to Jess. "I said to keep her outside."

"Oh, leave her alone, she just wants to spend time with her grandma."

Jess didn't know if it was the beer, the oily bread, or the arguing, but her stomach started to turn. She needed to be outside, away from the fussing. Just for a minute.

She went out into the front yard. The heat hit her, and she bent down by the grass, waiting to be sick.

After a couple of minutes, the wave of nausea passed, She saw something moving on the ground. It was the doodlebug, crawling up a blade of grass. Jess held out her hand. It hesitated, its antenna tickling her skin. Then it scuttled onto her palm.

She went back into the house, letting the critter scurry to her wrist.

Mom said, "She's heartsick about the way you turned out."

"Then let her tell me," Aunt Lou said. "Let her say whatever she wants. I don't get to choose her last words to me, but I wish I could. Maybe if you go first, you'll tell me how disappointing of a sister I was to you, but that won't be the last thing I say to you. It's not how I want us to end. Is that what you want? Is that what you really want for me and Momma?"

Rebecca, for the first time that Jess knew of, said nothing back. Then she scowled at the bug on her forearm. "Jessica, get that out of here."

"It's for Grandma."

Jess opened the door. Grandma wasn't exactly sitting up. She was propped up on pillows, but she was holding her head up better than before.

"Look what I found," Jess said, stepping towards the bed.

The doodlebug edged to the underside of her elbow. She touched it with her other hand, and it sprang into a ball. Jess collected it gently.

"Hold your hand out," Jess said to Grandma.

Jess tipped the pet onto her palm.

"What's this?" Grandma asked.

"I got a doodlebug for you. Wait a second. It'll open back up, remember?"

The doodlebug opened and tread uncertainly onto its new terrain.

Her mom and Aunt Lou were still arguing. The nurse excused herself. Grandma and Jess passed the doodlebug back and forth. Her grandmother wasn't acting like someone who would be dead soon, laughing like a small child.

Jess wanted to ask her if she ever prayed on all those rosaries. She wanted to ask if she ever regretted leaving the Convent. She thought about asking her if she was afraid to die. She almost told her that she loved her. She almost begged her to be sweet to Aunt Lou. She nearly asked her a question that she was too afraid to ask herself. *If I was like Aunt Lou, would you still love me?* Each time Jess opened her mouth to talk, nothing would come out. There was just this, them playing and laughing together. She didn't want any big, heavy talk to take that away.

It had been something big and heavy that had taken Grandma and Aunt Lou from each other.

Part Two
2014

2

Jess turned the "closed" sign to "open" and looked out of the storefront window into the quiet darkness. Flynn's Bakery didn't get many customers before sunrise, mostly nurses getting ready for their twelve-hour shifts or cashiers working overnight at the Walmart by the interstate. It would be around 8:00 that customers would order mugs of coffee and cinnamon rolls or croissants and open their laptops in one of the cushy red booths along the wall opposite the display counter.

Years before Aunt Lou had bought the building, it had been a cafe. She'd kept the cafe look of the place, with the booths along the wall, the yellow wooden tables, green chairs, and the original black and white tile flooring. Ceiling fans spun on their laziest settings. Aunt Lou and Vivienne liked to play old blues in the morning, like Jelly Roll Morton, Robert Johnson, and Bessie Smith. As the day went on, they would switch to folk or jazz. It was only when they'd close, and the very last customer was out that Aunt Lou would play heavy metal.

Jess loved the first hour of work. She would brew the coffee, pull the pastries and the breads from the oven, frost the cakes, and watch the sun stretch over the buildings across the street.

The silver bell on the door jingled as Jess's brother, Toby, came in carrying a strange potted plant. It had broad, green leaves, and the bloom was shaped like the side profile of a bird wearing an orange and purple headdress.

Toby was eight years younger than Jess and, in Jess's opinion, prettier. He had slender hands, deep brown eyes with long lashes, and a thick, dark, soft head of hair. As a kid, he'd been picked on for not having hair on his legs, which Jess had assured him didn't make him less of a boy. "Those assholes have got more hair than brains," she'd told him. "That doesn't make them more manly than you."

Sometimes, Jess saw the guys who'd picked on her brother walking down the street, or they'd come into the bakery to pick up a birthday cake for their kids. They weren't half as good-looking as the young man who walked towards her now.

Toby set the plant on the marble counter. "Trade a plant for a coffee?"

"Toby," said Jess. "What the hell is that?"

"I got it for Amber. I thought it was cool and weird, but she doesn't want it."

"I don't want it either."

"Can I still have coffee? And two of those muffins?"

Aunt Lou walked out of the kitchen and stood next to Jess, wiping her hands with a dishtowel. Her white apron was stained with butter and flour.

Louanne looked much the same as she had twenty years before, but with purple-spiked hair instead of blue. Jess only noticed that her aunt had aged when she looked at old pictures and saw how smooth her skin had been, and how less freckled her arms were. She had given up cigarettes, but not beer.

"Don't give that boy anything," she said.

"Aunt Lou," Toby whined.

"You can bring a coffee to your wife for putting up with you."

"I'm taking her camping today," he said. "I don't even like nature. Doesn't that score me some points?"

Aunt Lou leaned over the counter and tapped her cheek. He gave her a kiss, and she smiled like it was magic.

"What you want, baby?" she said.

"Strawberry basil muffins."

"What is that on my counter?"

"It's Jess's plant," Toby explained.

"It is not," Jess said. She pushed the silver button on the thermos and filled two large paper cups to the top. "But I think I know someone who would like it. When are you guys leaving?"

"In about an hour."

Jess set the coffees on the counter. "Why are you going camping? You're allergic to everything."

The last time he went camping, Toby had gotten stung by a bee, his throat closed up, and Amber had to take him to the emergency room.

He shrugged. "It was part of my vows. I promised her I'd go camping at least once a year. I've got Benadryl and my EpiPen, I'll be fine."

Jess moved the plant to the floor after he left.

"Why is he doing this to himself?" Jess asked. "How are they supposed to have a good time together if he goes into anaphylactic shock?"

"He's in love."

"Amber's not going to have the romantic experience she's hoping for if her husband is sick the whole time."

"I remember," Louanne said, mischief spreading across her face. "Years ago, Vivienne got so trashed one night, she fell into the laundry basket and thought it was the couch. She puked in the clothes. I had to help her rinse off in the shower."

"Ugh."

Louanne shrugged. "We still had sex."

Jess thought of the man she was currently divorcing. "That never would have happened with Alan."

"Doesn't sound like there was anything happening at all," Louanne said.

"No," Jess said. "Not in a couple of years. Want to hear something awful?"

"Always."

"I never liked sleeping with him. Even kissing him felt weird."

Jess had gotten together with Alan during their junior year of high school. She remembered thinking that he was cute, but what she'd really liked about him was that he was a good friend. It made her trust him and feel close to him. He'd been her first everything—first date, first kiss, first sex. It had been six months since they'd split up, after being together for eighteen years. The part that hurt the most was losing that sweet, good friend she'd spent half her life. Alan was angry now. Resentful. She didn't see the kind boy she'd fallen in love with years ago. Now when she saw him, which was only every other weekend when he came by to pick up the kids, he was quiet and cold. He'd started seeing someone else recently, and Jess was hoping that would chill him out, but it only seemed to make him more distant.

"Well," Louanne said. "Alan's still the only person you've ever been with."

"So?"

"So, you just need to find someone else to grease the wheels. What about that lesbian you got living next door to you?"

Pam, the lesbian in question, had been on Jess's mind. She hadn't said anything to Louanne about it yet. It wasn't that Aunt Lou would have a problem with it, it was just that the feelings were inconvenient.

"Pam isn't just 'some lesbian,'" she said. "She's my best friend."

"Girlfriend, more like."

"Why are you saying that?"

"Because y'all act like a couple."

"We do not act like a couple!"

Vivienne shouldered the door open, holding a pen to a folded newspaper. She used to open the shop with Louanne, but since she'd developed a restless leg problem that kept her up at night, Jess had taken over the early duties. Vivienne didn't mind because she'd never been a morning person. She and Louanne lived in the apartment above the shop, so she didn't even have to rush when she was finally up. She'd eat a little breakfast, grab the paper, and appear at the shop door scribbling letters into the crossword puzzle, her mane of curly red hair obscuring her face.

"Viv," Aunt Lou said. "Don't Jess and Pam act like a couple?"

"Yes," she said, frowning at the puzzle as she walked. "What's another word for 'think?'"

"Ponder?"

"Hmm. No." She set the paper on the counter and kissed Louanne on the cheek. "What's this about Jess and Pam?"

"That they're pretty much a couple."

"Oh yeah, that's true," Vivienne said.

"How?" Jess asked.

"You nap together," Vivienne pointed out.

"That was only once because we were tired."

Vivienne's eyes widened. "Contemplate!" she blurted out and reached for the puzzle.

The bell rang, and two customers walked in.

"All right, honey, look alive," Louanne said to Vivienne.

"I know, I know," she said, filling in the last couple of letters.

More customers arrived. Hospital workers in scrubs, men and women in blue Wal-Mart vests, and couples coming in to nibble on cinnamon rolls while they read the paper. The easy conversations with the customers gave Jess a cozy feeling. Jess started working at her Aunt Lou's bakery at seventeen, which at the time she'd done because it was convenient, but she'd come to love baking and the way the crankiest of guests would relax when she handed them a plate of something delicious. Even if Aunt Lou hadn't hired her, she would have become a baker.

The hours were good for her, too. She worked the first shift from 4:00 in the morning to 11:00. Pam was a teacher at her kids' grammar school. In the mornings, Pam drove their kids to school, and Jess picked up her two and Pam's daughter in the afternoons. Since it was July, Pam kept an eye on all of them during the day.

A few hours into her shift, Jess's curly-haired six-year-old Betsy ran to the pastry case and planted her hands on the glass. Her son, Kevin, and Pam's daughter, Alex, trailed behind her.

Kevin, who was tall for ten and the kind of skinny that made people want to feed him, looked like Jess, with his dark hair and deep brown eyes. Betsy looked more like the women on her father's side of the family. Light-haired, short, and stocky. Alex was Kevin's age. She looked just like her mother—honey-colored hair and playful green eyes. Pam had said that Alex was the result of a one-night stand, and the only time she had been with a man. She said it was like having a surprise sperm donor. But Alex looked so much like Pam it was easy to forget that she had a father at all.

"I want that one," Betsy said, patting the glass between her and a cherry cheese Danish.

"Did you save me a chocolate muffin?" Kevin asked.

"If you only have one, you should give it to me," Alex told her.

"But I'm her favorite," Kevin said, shoving Alex with no real force.

Alex covered Kevin's face with the palm of her hand and beamed at Jess. "Ignore this plebian. The muffin, please."

"Plebian" was a word Alex had recently learned and used as often as she could, usually against Kevin.

"Don't serve this rude peasant," Kevin mumbled through Alex's fingers.

"You're both nuts," Jess said.

Pam walked in. She brushed her bangs from her eyes and smiled at Jess.

Aunt Lou's voice boomed from the kitchen. "What's all that racket?" She appeared holding three spoonsful of green icing and looking around the dining area in confusion.

"It's me," Betsy announced.

Aunt Lou looked down as if recognizing Betsy for the first time. "I thought that might be you. I'm glad you're here. I have a lot of leftover icing. Can you help me throw it away?"

Betsy giggled. "Let me eat it!"

"All right, come on." Aunt Lou held out the spoons, and each child took one. "I've got a whole tub back there, so pace yourself."

"You are *not* eating a whole tub of icing," Jess told them.

"Your momma's not the boss," Aunt Lou whispered to the kids.

Vivienne came out of the kitchen. "Are those my babies, I hear?"

"Yes," Betsy said.

"Miss Betsy," Vivienne said. She bent down and gave her a hug. "I think it's about time for a coffee break. Don't you, Lou?"

"I think you're right. I'll brew you three tall ones and we'll have coffee. Sound good?"

Jess shook her head at Pam while Aunt Lou steamed the milk for three café au laits that the children would load up with sugar.

"Why must she jack them up on caffeine?" Pam asked Jess.

"At least it's not beer and cigarettes," Jess said. "Not yet, anyway. We need to keep an eye on that woman in about five years."

Pam crossed her arms and pressed herself against the glass, staring through the top of it. Her face and hair glowed in the light of the pastry case. Her green eyes became vibrant. Everyone, Jess thought, looked holy in the pastry case light, but Pam was the most angelic. Pam took her time picking something out while Aunt Lou got a tray of the kids' breakfast and brought it to their table.

"One of those," Pam said, pointing to the tray of lemon bars.

Jess picked out the best-looking one and set it on a plate. Pam joined the aunts and the kids at their table.

Brett, a broad-shouldered customer whose order Jess had memorized, came shouldering a messenger bag. He told her hello with half-open eyes.

"Morning, Brett," she said, filling a large paper cup. "You're not burning up in that sweater? It's supposed to get up to ninety degrees today."

"The school's cold," he said with a yawn. "I was up grading papers."

Jess asked him how his classes were going, and he filled her in while she fished a blueberry croissant out of the case and got his coffee. Brett taught history at a local university, and Jess liked hearing his stories about what lame excuses his students would give him about missing class.

"Next time, lose sleep doing something fun," she told him, passing him the bag.

He grinned and stepped towards the door but then paused. "Would you want to have dinner with me sometime?"

The surprise of the question must have been all over Jess's face because he said, "I would understand if you can't. I know you're getting divorced."

"Yeah," she said. "My kids are over there. Have you met them?"

"Oh," he said, his eyes fully opening. He asked her which ones were hers. "Well, why don't I leave you my number? If you change your mind just give me a call."

He handed her his card, took his coffee and muffin, and left. Jess stared at it, and Pam stepped up to the counter, looking at it with her. "He asked you out."

"Yeah. Do people usually give you their business cards when they ask you to dinner? Feels awfully formal. But then the last time I got asked out was in the eleventh grade when Alan got his best friend to ask me for him."

"Are you going to call him?" Pam asked.

"I don't want to."

"Do you like him?"

Jess paid attention to the way that Pam asked the question. It was nonchalant, like she was genuinely curious but not invested in the answer.

"I like him in general," Jess said. "I don't want to go out with him."

"You smiled a lot with him."

"He's a customer. Hey. I have something for you."

Jess lifted the plant and placed it in front of Pam.

"A bird of paradise," Pam said.

"Toby gave it to me. I had a feeling you might like it."

"Yeah, look at it. It's so weird." She moved one of the long flower petals up and down like a bottom jaw, making it talk. "Good morning, Jess. I am weird, but I am beautiful."

"You're crazy. So, you want it?"

"Yes. Thank you."

"Can you still help me with the yard sale tomorrow?"

"Yeah."

That night, Jess dreamed about Pam's hair shining golden in the light of the pastry case. She wanted to touch it, but every time she reached out to her, her grandmother would come through the door, alive and wanting a muffin. Then her mother. Then her kids. Then Alan. There were always just so many people to think about.

૬ ૬ ૬

Jess and her kids lived in the middle of a cul-de-sac, in a three-bedroom, two-bath house with a red door. The red door was the one feature that set her house apart from the others on her block, which were all one-story structures that Jess thought were all shaped like giant bricks— rectangular, with nearly flat roofs. It was a neighborhood of cul-de-sacs all named after (and all stemming from) one main road in their small town.

The house's selling point had been the backyard's size, which was almost a quarter of an acre. They'd bought it when Kevin was four, and Betsy was a baby. She thought that when the kids were older, they could play volleyball, soccer, or throw a football in the space. Three Magnolia trees lined the back of the yard, ready for the kids to climb when their arms and legs were strong enough.

When Betsy and Kevin were small, Jess had been happy with the quiet of the neighborhood. The only sounds from the street were kids on bicycles, cars drifting in and out of their driveways, and the garbage truck that came on Tuesdays and Fridays. Now, as Jess steered her wheelbarrow between the two white folding tables in her driveway, she wished it had more traffic. She'd forgotten to advertise the yard sale, and there wasn't hope of much foot traffic.

The yard sale was something that she was excited about at first. She would be getting rid of things and making a little bit of cash, but it turned out that deciding how much the unwanted things cost and expecting people to pay it stressed her out. Jess would ask Pam if she thought she'd priced things fairly. She had hoped that by now, Pam would be walking across the yard sipping coffee. But not yet.

She set the wheelbarrow down at the foot of the empty street. She wondered if anyone would buy it with the word "GROOM" painted on the side. It had been one of the more creative gifts at her wedding shower. A bunch of friends had filled the wheelbarrow with man presents—a tool set, a garden hose, a saw, and a pair of yellow scruffy gloves like big paws. They'd given Jess a "BRIDE" laundry basket loaded with cleaning supplies. Since her and Alan's separation, Jess had done both the yard work and the housework. She wore both the big paw gloves and the yellow latex ones that were just like the ones she'd gotten in the BRIDE basket.

Jess inspected the tables. They were strewn with toy ponies, books, power tools she couldn't identify, a long lighter, Beanie Babies, piles of dishes, and other breakables she didn't need anymore. She considered taking her old track shoes off the table, but her house was cluttered enough. As much as it bothered her to let go of that part of her life, back when she had boundless energy, she had to throw them away if no one took them.

She swept her dark bangs away from her eyes. The sun peeked through gray clouds passing overhead. They looked lost, like they were scheduled to be in a storm somewhere, and were hurriedly on their way to find it.

"Good," she told them. "Keep moving."

Kevin walked out of the garage with a box of old vases, ones that Alan had brought her home from the grocery store with a single rose in them every Valentine's Days.

"Do we have to sell that?" he asked, nodding at the GROOM wheelbarrow.

"Yes," said Jess, taking the box from him and setting it on the table with plates and other glass objects.

"But Dad took me for rides in it," Kevin said. "It's fun. Here, get in, I'll show you."

"No," Jess said. "I want to sell everything we don't need, and we don't need that as a mode of transportation."

"Okay," Kevin said.

He gripped the handles and fell silent.

"What are you thinking about?" Jess asked.

"Dad says I'm getting too old to play like a kid."

"You are a kid."

"How old are you when you're not a kid?"

"That's a good question. I don't think you automatically go from child to adult. There are stages. And you're never too old to have fun."

Kevin raised his eyebrows and the wheel barrel. "So, ride?"

"Good try. No."

Betsy walked up with an armful of seashells, and they clattered to the ground when she reared her head back to sneeze.

"What's this for?" asked Jess.

"To sell!" Betsy announced, sweeping her arm across her nose.

Jess wiped it with a balled-up tissue from her pocket. Then she looked over her shoulder at the next yard. Still no Pam.

"Betsy, knock on Miss Pam's door and ask her if she still wants to do the sale with us. Tell her we're starting."

Betsy scurried over to the house next door as Mr. Howard rolled up on his bike. Mr. Howard was in his mid-sixties and rode an enormous tricycle with a basket on the front. The basket carried a portable cassette player that blared "Love Me Tender."

"Good morning," Mr. Howard said, blinking a lot. He stepped gingerly off the bike, and hitched up his tan shorts. "Well, now. What have we got today?"

"My childhood," said Kevin, with exaggerated gravity.

"Ignore him," Jess said.

"Got any Fix-a-Flat?" Mr. Howard asked.

"I don't think so," said Jess.

"Shucks. I could always use some."

Thunder rumbled above them.

"You might get rained out," Mr. Howard said, pointing to the clouds.

"But there's sunshine."

"Don't matter," he said. "You know summer storms."

Lindsey, a neighbor with purple biking shorts and a pink sports bra, walked up the driveway. She sipped a green, frozen concoction from a glass. Sweat glistened on her face, chest, and tanned abs.

"Hey, Lindsey," Jess said, greeting her, thinking about her own stomach muscles buried beneath flab and stretch marks.

Lindsey waved back and asked Jess if she was going to sign Betsy up for Girl Scouts in the fall. Jess said she probably would, but she wasn't thinking about that as she spoke. Instead, she was contemplating why she was selling her old running shoes.

When she ran track in high school, she loved sprinting—keeping perfectly still and then exploding across the track. It made her feel strong to move so fast. She didn't need a car or a bicycle to get her anywhere. Just two feet and a good pair of shoes.

She hadn't worn them in years.

"You're coming to the party tonight, right?" Lindsey asked.

"I'm not sure," said Jess.

Lindsey took a sip and said with her teeth on the straw, "The kids are invited too. You don't have to worry about getting a sitter. Better take a look at this stuff before the rain comes, huh? Oo, I need a wheelbarrow."

Kevin climbed inside of it. "You can have it if you give me a ride around the yard."

"It's thirty dollars," Jess said.

"I'll give you twenty-five," Lindsey countered.

"Fifteen and three rides up and down the street," said Kevin.

"Ten dollars, and you get to keep this child," Jess told Lindsey.

"Oh my," Lindsey said.

Alex streaked across the yard on her scooter with Betsy chasing after her. Pam followed, carrying a coffee mug in each hand.

"Mornin'," Pam said to Lindsey, handing Jess one of the mugs. "So what are you buying, Lindsey? Everything?"

"I'm trying to convince Jess to come to the party tonight. Maybe you'll have better luck."

"Of course, we're going to go," said Pam. She looked to Jess.

"We are?" Jess asked.

"Free food and kid-friendly? Why would we not?"

Jess sipped the coffee Pam had given her. "This is perfect."

Pam smiled. "You fix your coffee just like your aunt. Add sugar past the point that feels reasonable."

Lindsey tsk'ed. "That's like my husband with cheese."

Pam set her mug on the table, yawned, and stretched her arms as high as they could go. Jess liked it when Pam stretched high like that, her long torso tightening like a bowstring, her breasts lifting.

Jess began arranging Beanie Babies in a line on the table. She'd never really wanted them. Her grandmother had given her one every Christmas and birthday until she died. Now, they glared up at her with accusatory looks as she displayed them along with the other things she'd never wanted.

Lindsey handed Pam cash and took two vases.

"I hope y'all come by," Lindsey said. "You're two of the only people we invited that I like having around."

"How much did I make?" Jess asked after Lindsey left.

"Two whole dollars," Pam said.

"Fantastic. And two less things in my garage."

There was a flash of light, and a second later, the thunder came.

"Dammit," Jess muttered.

"You sure you don't have any Fix-a-Flat?" Mr. Howard asked.

"I might," said Pam.

Mr. Howard rubbed his hands together as Pam headed next door to her garage.

Alex stepped off of her scooter and let it fall to the grass. "Why are you in the wheelbarrow?" she asked Kevin.

"I don't want anyone to take it."

"Can I push you?"

"Push us both!" cried Betsy.

Kevin scooched over in the bucket to make room for his sister. Alex gripped the handles to steady the thing as Betsy climbed into it.

"Oh no, guys, come on," Jess said.

Betsy pointed to a tan, full-sized truck that turned into the cul-de-sac.

"It's Daddy!" she said.

Alan's F-250 pulled up on the side of the road, and he stepped out of it. He wasn't a tall man, and the size of the truck dwarfed him. He had sandy hair thinning at the temples and small, tight facial features that came together to draw attention to the point of his nose. In fact, Jess had always thought that his face needed glasses sitting large on the tip of his slightly upturned nose.

Kevin silently slid down a little in his seat. Betsy drummed her feet in the wheelbarrow. "Come push us, Daddy."

"Not now, sweetheart," he told her. "I have to talk to Mom."

Alan nodded at Mr. Harold, who nodded back and then began picking things up from a table, inspecting them, and setting them down. Jess knew he was listening.

"I just got your message," Alan said, tightly.

"Which one?"

Alan opened his arms. "About this. Why didn't you wait for me to come get my stuff before you sold everything? Look," he said, pointing at his circular saw. "This is mine, I bought this."

"How often did you use it?" Jess asked.

"That's not the point," he said. "You have no right to sell it without my permission."

"Do I have your permission?"

"And this!" he exclaimed, dashing over to the food processor on the table.

"Alan," said Jess, in a way that suggested he'd never processed food in his life.

"This is my stuff."

"Your stuff?"

"Partly mine."

Jess closed her eyes as lightning flashed. "I called you twice this week. I left messages telling you that you should come get what you wanted before I sold it. You didn't call back."

Alan said he had been too busy to even listen to her messages until that morning and was appalled; he never would have sold their things without her consent, and the Jess he'd married wouldn't have dreamed of selling the stuff they'd bought together. He stammered as he said, "our stuff." He cradled the food processor in his arms as if it were one of the children Jess was trying to sell.

Pam held out a can of Fix-a-Flat to Mr. Howard. "Is this what you need?"

Mr. Howard brightened. "How much?"

"Ten bucks," Pam told him.

"That's too much," Alan said. "You can't charge him that."

Mr. Howard assured Alan that it was okay, and handed over the cash. He stashed the can in his basket next to his boom box and rode away just as "Blue Suede Shoes" began to play.

"You can't sell something that you got from my house," Alan told her.

"It's from my garage," Pam said.

"Leave her alone, Alan."

Jess wanted to say that she didn't understand his problem. He wasn't hurting for money, and he had a girlfriend. Why did he need to bother her about things like an old food processor? But he'd never really liked Pam, even though she'd always been nice to him. It made Jess wonder if he knew how she'd felt about Pam since the moment she'd moved next door.

"Dad?" Kevin said.

He and Betsy, nestled in the wheelbarrow, locked their eyes on Alan. Drops of rain hit Jess's shoulders.

"Alan, if you want some of this stuff, take it," said Jess. "I'm going to have to postpone. If you want half of what I make, that's fine."

"I don't want the money," he said, like she had insulted him. "But you can't sell this..."

He loaded the circular saw into the cab of his truck. Then he took the drill, the Allen wrenches, the baseball glove, the sander, and the food processor. He told the kids he'd call them later. He drove off without looking even looking at Jess.

What did she expect? A friendly hug? I love yous and take cares? They had only been separated for six months.

Rain pelted them. Pam ushered the kids inside, ineffectively covering them with her arms.

The rain darkened the pretty blues and yellows of the Beanie Babies, and filled the vases drop by drop. Jess took her track shoes and left the rest.

3

The anniversary party was a barbecue. The back patio was decorated with red balloons floating up from two tables of food, and streamers of hearts hung from the patio roof. Sweaty neighborhood kids jumped and pushed each other in a red, blue, and yellow bounce house in the yard. The Top 40 station blared from a speaker by the back door and middle-aged guests in a variety of crimson shorts, shirts, dresses, and flip-flops grabbed cans of beer from a line of coolers along the blonde brick wall of the house. Jess felt like she was at a Valentine's Day Dance at high school where only the teachers showed up.

Jess didn't know what to talk about with her peers who stood around her, chatting easily. She, not understanding from the invitation that there was a red theme, wore blue. The sun was going down, but the heat from the day felt like it was coming up from the ground, and the smoke from the grill at the edge of the patio stung her nose and eyes.

She was relieved when Lindsey walked through the back door in her red, ruffled shirt and white shorts.

"Happy anniversary," Jess said.

"You came," said Lindsey.

Jess wondered how Lindsey's hair kept its sprayed, stiff curls in this humidity. Other women just seemed to know how to do things like that.

"You didn't wear red," Lindsey said.

"I didn't realize there was a theme."

"Yes, ma'am! Twenty years and still hot." Lindsey, quoting the line from the invitation, held her arms out, and shook her chest.

Jess pulled at the neck of her T-shirt. "It was clean."

Lindsey excused herself to go talk to an older woman in a red tutu. Pam, who'd had the presence of mind to wear maroon, stepped through the crowd next to Jess. Pam's bangs kinked in the heat. Jess wanted to loop one of the ringlets with her finger but kept her hands at her sides.

"The kids are good in the bounce house," Pam said. "Kevin and Alex are bouncing Betsy ten feet high."

"That should make her happy."

"It is."

"Wish we could go in there with them," said Jess. "I never know what to say to people at these things."

"What's to say?" Pam asked. "Eat a hamburger, get a margarita, wish them twenty more years, and get out."

"They have margaritas?"

"Yeah, over there." Pam pointed to a table against the wall lined with booze and mixers.

"Well, shit."

Jess went to the table but stopped when she saw Alan and his girlfriend, Cindy, standing beside it. Cindy had white-blonde hair, dark eyebrows, pale skin, and wore a little red dress. Alan wore a tomato-colored shirt that made his face look purple. He poured white wine into a plastic cup, and passed it to Cindy.

Lindsey took Jess's arm. "Hey, Tom invited Alan. I'm sorry, I didn't think to tell him not to. You want me to ask them to leave?"

"No," said Jess. "It's fine. He was your neighbor, too."

"I can't believe he brought her," Lindsey said, shaking her head.

"Want me to go get you that margarita?" Pam asked.

"No, I can go get it myself. He's not going to yell at me here. Besides, it's time I met the woman my kids see every other weekend."

"Hey," Jess said to them.

Cindy lowered her drink and gave Jess the same smile that she was giving everyone she didn't know. Alan fumbled with his cup.

"I didn't know you were coming," he said.

"I live across the street, remember? You were there a few hours ago."

"I know."

"Our kids are friends with Lindsey's kids."

"I know, Jess."

Cindy gave a smile that was more like a facial tick. "You're Jess."

"I am."

"I'm Cindy," she said, extending a hand. "Your kids are wonderful."

Your boyfriend kisses like a dying fish, Jess thought, accepting Cindy's small hand.

"So, the kids are here?" Alan asked.

"They're in the bounce house."

Alan said to Cindy, "Let's go say hi," touched her lower back and guided her towards the spacewalk.

The last time Alan had embraced her, she had been doing the dishes. She'd felt his hands slide around her waist and his breath on top of her shoulder before he pressed his wet lips against it and gave her a noisy kiss. She'd cringed and then felt guilty about reacting that way, so she let him keep touching her.

"How'd that go?" Pam asked.

"Fine."

Pam studied her. "You don't look fine."

"She fits," said Jess, as Cindy slid an arm around Alan's waist. Jess never embraced him like that. "She just fits with him, doesn't she?"

Pam glanced at Cindy. "Should we warn her that he's always late with the child support?" Jess laughed and Pam said, "Did you feel like you didn't fit with him?"

"No, I never did. I didn't think much of it when we got married. I never felt like I fit anywhere, so I was used to that feeling. Even now, I feel like I'm the only weird one here."

"I'm standing right here, you know."

"Yeah, but you're normal. You even knew what to wear."

"That's because I read the invitation."

"There were too many hearts on that thing to make out actual words."

"Everybody's weird, Jess. Everybody has their thing."

"Yeah? What's her thing?" Jess pointed to a woman in a red Polo shirt and a white tennis hat.

"She's into leather."

Jess nodded to a bald man with red shorts and a T-shirt with a trout on it. "What about him?"

"He and his wife can only have sex if they're dressed like cats."

"Stop."

"See what happens if you meow."

They snickered. Pam's rubbed Jess's upper back. "You're not any weirder than anyone else. It's just a hard time."

Jess dropped her shoulders at the touch and leaned into it.

Alex was teaching Kevin how to do a cartwheel while the spacewalk jerked with hopping children behind them.

Alex raised her arms. "You just go like this and, like..." her face scrunched up in thought. "You just throw yourself over."

She'd said, "Throw yourself," but Kevin thought the execution of the stunt was much more graceful than that. Alex took one step and was upside down, hands on the earth, her feet arcing above her to land square in the ground. And then she was right side up again, hands in the air. He thought she was like a palindrome, ending the same way she began.

His dad stepped next to him with his hands on his hips. "What are you guys up to?"

"Alex is teaching me how to cartwheel," Kevin said.

"Cartwheels are for girls," Alan said. "Why don't you do a flip?"

"How's a flip different from a cartwheel?" Kevin asked.

"I can teach you how to flip," Cindy said.

Alan smiled at her in a way that made Kevin uncomfortable. "Show him, honey."

"I can't. I'm in a dress."

"I know."

"Can you show me how to flip?" Betsy asked Cindy.

"Sure," Cindy told her. "Next time you're at your dad's."

"And paint my nails again," Betsy said.

"Do you know how to flip?" Kevin asked his dad.

"No," said Alan. "I was never into that stuff."

"I am," Kevin said. "I want to be a cheerleader when I get to high school."

He didn't. He just really wanted to bother Alan.

"Don't do that," Alan said, looking grim.

"Why not? It's really athletic."

"Lots of boys are cheerleaders," Alex said.

"It's true," said Cindy.

"Thank you, Cindy," Kevin said. "If you don't mind, I would also like to paint my nails with you and Betsy."

Betsy clapped and cheered. Cindy said she'd be delighted.

"He's messing with you," Alan told Cindy. He frowned at Kevin. "Very funny, son."

Alan took Cindy's hand and led her away.

Betsy tore through the crowd and slammed into Jess. She lifted her face and grinned wide. "I saw Dad!"

"Nice surprise, huh?"

"Yes, and Cindy said she would paint my nails when I come over again."

Pam pulled two red plastic cups from the tall stack on the table. "Salt or no salt?"

"Whatever, just make it a double," Jess replied.

Alex ran up behind Betsy and tickled her until she fell on the ground, paralyzed with laughter.

Kevin walked up with his hands in his pockets. He reminded Jess of a contemplative, older man. "Why did Dad bring Cindy?" he asked.

"She's Dad's date," Jess said. "She seems nice."

"She is. Dad just acts weird around her."

"How so?"

"Like he's showing off in front of her."

"Here," said Pam, passing Jess a cup filled with ice and a golden mixture.

Jess took a sip that shocked the insides of her mouth.

"Geez, Pam," said Jess, turning the cup around in her hands.

"You said you wanted a kick."

"Why does Momma need a kick?" Betsy asked, standing up and dusting off her jumper.

"Because sometimes she needs one," Pam said, raising her leg at the knee to boot Jess in the pants.

Jess returned the kick, but began to lose her balance and set her drink down on a nearby table. She hopped, landing with one foot forward and one foot back, held up her hands, fingers straight and tight together like knives to chop Pam's arm, and Pam stepped forward and soft-punched Jess's stomach. Jess made a fist to return the blow, but she laughed so hard that she grazed Pam's stomach with her knuckles.

Kevin tilted his head back and sighed. Alex recognized the exasperation in that sigh. It was the frustration she felt when her mom wasn't paying attention to something important.

"What's the matter?" Alex asked.

Kevin nodded towards the yard where the kids were, further away from the adults. When they were out of earshot, Kevin said, "I don't think Dad likes me."

"Your dad likes you," Alex said. "He was just aggravated because he knew you were messing with him."

"That's true. It's also just weird having both Mom and Dad here, but not together."

"I guess that would be weird," Alex said. "We don't have to hang around them. Come on. Let's go ask Mr. Tom if we can light the grill."

She and Kevin went to the barbecue pit, and Betsy trailed after them.

Jess took a long pull from her cup. She rattled the ice around and saw that there wasn't much left, so she drained it. She held the cup out to Pam. "Can you make another one just like that?"

Pam obliged. They continued their game of pointing out neighbors and guessing their secrets. The head of the PTA was a kleptomaniac who liked to steal lip gloss. The guy who always threw a neighborhood Super Bowl party had a Hello Kitty collection. A couple in matching red T-shirts were sleeping with their lawn guy.

"What do you think Lindsey and Tom are into?" Jess asked and took a sip.

Pam thought about it. "Bondage. Definitely. And Tom wants acrylic nails."

Jess snorted. "I need to find the bathroom."

"You drank too fast."

Jess stuck her tongue out at Pam and handed her the cup.

She spun towards the house. A warm, woozy feeling washed over her, and she walked through the French doors in a cloud. The living room reminded her of the church she'd gone to as a child with high cathedral ceilings. She made her way through the room using the back of the sectional couch for balance.

Pictures of Lindsey and Tom's two sons were in the hallway outside the bathroom. She thought of the school pictures of her own children and was hit with a sudden guilt that she'd gotten drunk while they were under her watch. She pushed open the bathroom door and pulled her cell phone out of her back pocket.

"Jess?" Pam answered. "Are you calling me from the bathroom?"

"I am. Listen, are the kids okay?"

"Yeah, they're fine."

"I've never been drunk in front of them before."

"Well, you're not in front of them right now. You're in front of a toilet."

"That doesn't make me feel better."

"They're okay, I promise. They're starting fires with Tom. I'll come in the house with you."

Jess clumsily managed to do what she needed to do, and came out of the bathroom to find Pam standing in the hallway with her arms folded. Jess ran a fingertip along one of her arms. Pam stiffened but didn't stop her.

"You look so serious," said Jess.

"Just sober."

Jess glanced at the slightly opened door at the end of the hall. "You think we're right about Lindsey and Tom?"

"What, that they've got a ball gag and chains in their room?"

"Yeah." Jess took Pam's hand and went towards the door. "Come on."

"We can't go in their room."

"Why not? Our purses are in there."

It was easy to pull Pam down the hall. Even with her protests, she tumbled along with her. Jess pushed the door open to a lamp-lit room. The king-sized bed was covered in purses, diaper bags, and backpacks.

Pam closed the door behind them, and Jess got belly-down on the floor. She lifted the bed skirt and stuck her head into the dark space.

"Jess, we can't," Pam started to say, and then stopped. "What's under there?"

"Ugh, nothing," she said with her head still under the box spring. "Not even dust."

"That's not possible," Pam said and bear-crawled across the floor to peek under the bed next to Jess. "This is cleaner than my entire house."

"How does she keep it like that?"

"She's got one of those robot vacuum cleaners."

Jess pushed through her foggy brain to think about it. "And Tom helps out. I've seen him do the dishes."

"Fuck."

"I know."

"Hey," Pam said, nudging her elbow against Jess's. "Why do you want to find something freaky about Lindsey and Tom?"

"I guess I just want to know if they are what they seem to be."

The heat that had consumed her before the icy margaritas came sweeping back across her face. Jess looked away from Pam and caught a glimpse of something black dangling underneath the corner of the bed near her right. She reached out and pulled a leather strap towards her.

"Pam," she said, brandishing it before her.

Pam squinted. "What is that?"

"It's a leather strap," said Jess, excitedly.

They scrambled out from under the bed. Jess pulled at where it connected beneath the box spring and unraveled the strap to its full length. It was about as long as her arm, with a cuff at the end. Pam ran to the other side of the bed and dug underneath the mattress.

"I found the other one," she exclaimed, pulling an identical strap from that side.

They ran to the other corners and found the same.

"Holy crap," said Jess. "How does this even work?"

"You've never been tied down before?" Pam asked.

"No. Have you?" she asked. "You got a contraption like this at home, or something?"

Pam smiled at the floor. "No. But I've done it before. It's fun."

Jess gasped and slapped her on the arm with the strap. "With who?"

"No one you know. It was ages ago."

"Were you the one tied down, or did you tie her down?"

"Jess."

She nudged Pam again. "Tell me."

"Both."

"How long has it been since you had a girlfriend?"

"Long time," Pam said. "You know how it is. It's not easy with a kid. Or in this town. Besides your aunts, it's like a queer desert."

"Do you miss it?"

"What?" Pam asked.

"Sex."

"Sometimes. I miss kissing more than anything."

"I never liked kissing."

Pam laughed. "You've only kissed men. That's why. Just my opinion, but I'm biased."

Jess had never stood so close to Pam before. Her heart charged like she was sprinting, but she was standing still. Jess closed the space between them. Her fingertips slid against Pam's cheek until she held her face in her hand. She brushed her lips against Pam's and felt Pam gasp. Jess marveled at how soft Pam's lips were as they breathed into each other. Then they relaxed into a kiss that was so gentle it was almost not a kiss. Kissing Pam was like being connected with a part of her own body that had been missing. *I want to be the bride and groom of you,* she thought.

The doorknob rattled.

"Mom," said Kevin. The doorknob shook again. "Are you in there?"

Jess stepped back from Pam and dropped her hands to her sides. She took shaky, irregular breaths, as if her body didn't know what to do.

"I'm here," Jess answered.

"Can I come in?"

"I didn't lock the door," Jess whispered to Pam. "Did you?"

Pam nodded.

Jess moved quickly across the room and opened the door to her frown-faced son.

"Can we go home now?" he asked.

"Aren't you having a good time?"

Kevin shook his head. "It's too weird with Dad here."

Jess hugged him. Pam stepped beside her.

"Do you mind if we go?" Jess asked her.

They stared into each other as they had before, but Jess was filled with a different kind of nervousness. She was afraid to leave the room, as if stepping out of the door would undo what had just happened.

"That's probably a good idea," Pam said.

᠀᠀᠀

After Jess put the kids to bed, there was a timid knock on the door.

"Can I come in for a second?" Pam asked, with her hands in her back pockets.

Jess stepped aside. "You want some coffee?"

"It's 9:00 at night."

"Well, I thought tequila might be a bad idea."

Pam took a step closer to Jess. Pam's arms, bent to keep her hands in her back pockets, trembled and her breath shook as she said, "I don't think it was a bad idea."

Jess could smell her. It was a scent she couldn't describe—it was just Pam. But it was so much more than "just Pam." Breathing her in was like that feeling she'd get with a first bite of cake. It was to be savored with her eyes closed.

"I don't think so either," Jess said. "Did I kiss okay?"

"It was as wonderful as I thought it might be."

"You've thought about kissing me before?"

"All the time," Pam said. "I just didn't know if you'd want to."

"All the time," Jess said.

Pam wrapped her arms around Jess. Jess lay her cheek on Pam's chest, closed her eyes, and felt the rhythm of Pam's heartbeat—the rise and fall of her breath. Jess kissed the bare skin above the neck of the tank top. Pam kissed the top of Jess's head, then her temple, her cheek, and then found Jess's mouth. This kiss was deeper than the first, their tongues touching, their bodies pressed together, and Jess's hands in Pam's hair.

Pam pressed her fingers against Jess's lips to separate them. They held one another, breathing.

"How would we work?" Pam asked.

"I don't know. Would you want to try?" As she said it out loud, Jess realized how much she wanted the answer to be yes.

"I do," Pam said. "But the kids."

"Kevin's so confused."

"Alex adores him. And Betsy. And I don't want to lose you."

Jess squeezed her tight. "So don't."

"I should go. Alex is by herself, and I told her I would just be a minute. Come over tomorrow?"

Jess nuzzled into Pam's chest again. "Yes."

ɚ ɚ ɚ

Jess set the pot on the edge of the garden. Pam was on her knees, digging with a small spade.

"Don't put it there," Pam said.

"Why not?"

"Birds of paradise get big. They need to be six feet apart."

Pam had loved the plant so much that she bought a second one. Her garden, which ran along the fence, was colorful with impatiens, marigolds, black-eyed Susans, and a small bush of yellow knock-out roses. Jess moved to the other side of the garden, feeling the distance. They both stabbed into the ground. After a few minutes sweat rolled off the tip of Jess's nose.

"We should plant tomatoes," Jess said.

"Tomatoes?"

"And lettuce and stuff."

"You want to plant a salad?" Pam asked.

"Yeah, we could have fresh vegetables. If we got chickens roosting, I could make you quiches."

"That would be amazing. But I like to grow the pretty stuff." Pam touched the beak of the bird of paradise as if it were something fragile and precious. "You're thinking like a baker."

"Oh," Jess laughed at herself. "I guess I think about food when I'm nervous."

"Are you nervous?" Pam asked.

Jess stopped digging and pulled one of her gloves off. She held out her hand, palm down, to show how it trembled.

Pam sat back on her haunches and rested her dirty gloves on her knees. "I like kissing you. I don't know what to do about it."

"I like kissing you too," Jess said.

Strands of hair lay wet against Pam's temples. Flecks of dirt dotted her forearms and neck. Pam was earth and heat. Jess watched a drop of sweat roll down Pam's collarbone. She had the impulse to catch it with her tongue. Jess had never wanted to taste someone as much as she did in that moment.

"Have you ever been attracted to a woman before?" Pam asked.

Jess nodded. "When I was fourteen, I had a crush on my gym teacher."

Pam laughed. "Of course you did."

"Ms. Harper," Jess said. "She was more than just pretty. She was nice. To everyone. She was the kind of teacher that a girl could talk to if she was pregnant. There was a rumor that she was gay, and some people made fun of her. Never to her face, but some people did. Hell, even I did. I think it was around Christmas that my mom reported her to the school."

"Why?"

"A parent found out that her roommate was her girlfriend. She was a lesbian at an all-girls Catholic school. She was supposed to live up to Catholic morals, which I didn't get. A bunch of my teachers were divorced, but they weren't fired for it. Mom asked if Ms. Harper had ever touched me. I told her no, but it didn't make a difference. Ms. Harper didn't come back after Christmas break."

"I'm sorry," Pam said. "Sometimes I'm afraid other parents will think the same thing of me."

"Thank God it's not 1995 anymore."

"We're not too far removed. Is that why you never tried with women?"

"Yeah. I think I was more bisexual when I was younger. I know that doesn't make sense, but I was attracted to Alan at one point. I had a lot of incentive to focus on him. At that time, most of my family wasn't talking to Aunt Lou."

"I probably would choose guys too."

"Pam," Jess said. Her teeth knocked together. She rubbed the sweat from her eyes and steadied herself. "Let's not cook tonight."

"Why?"

"I want to go on a date with you."

"What about the kids?"

"I can ask Aunt Lou and Viv if they'll watch them."

"That's not what I mean. What if it didn't work?"

"Then we won't eat together again."

"Come on, Jess."

"I just know," Jess said, "that I want to take you to dinner."

4

Jess and Pam sat across from each other on the patio at Bruning's, a seafood restaurant that sat alongside the dock of Lake Pontchartrain. Sailboats slipped out from the harbor, some with electric white lights along the cabins. The blue of the sky was dimming just enough for the lights to stand out so that out of the corner of Jess's eye, the boats looked like they wore strands of diamonds.

"Are you sure I'm dressed okay?" Jess asked her, smoothing her skirt down her legs.

She looked over at the other guests in their jean-shorts and T-shirts. In her slacks and white blouse, Pam looked dressed for one of the boats on the water.

"Of course," Pam said. "Why?"

"I wasn't sure if you'd like me in a skirt."

"I see you in skirts all the time. You look beautiful."

"So, what do we do?" asked Jess.

"Order food."

"We just order food like normal?"

Pam raised an eyebrow at her. "Yeah, crazy. It's dinner. We've had dinner together before."

"I know."

"It's the same procedure."

"Not exactly."

"How do you figure?"

"Because this time, I can kiss you when I want to."

Pam's smile crept slowly across her face. "The rules of consent still apply here."

"Fair enough."

Pam opened her menu, hiding her face.

"Do you not consent to being looked at?" Jess asked.

"Not at the moment. This is the part of the date where we decide what to order."

Jess picked up the menu. "I'll have one of everything. You're paying."

"*You* asked *me* out. So, you're paying."

"Is that how this works? The last time I had a first date was in the eleventh grade."

Pam's eyes widened.

"You knew that," Jess said.

"Yeah, I just hadn't thought about it that way."

The waiter came and took their wine orders. Brett, the professor, took a seat at a table across from her with a couple of other men.

"Jess?" he said, getting up from his chair. "Well, hey. So, this is what you look like when you're not covered in flour?"

Jess laughed uncomfortably. "Yeah."

"You look great." He extended his hand to Pam. "Hey, I'm Brett. I'm the guy who bothers her for breakfast every morning."

"Pam."

"What are you guys up to?" he asked.

"Well," said Jess. She looked to Pam for an answer, but Pam gave her a blank stare. "We needed a girl's night out."

"I gotcha. You still have my number, right?"

"Yes."

"Call me," he said.

He touched her shoulder. Jess flinched.

"I'm sorry," said Jess.

"That's not your fault," Pam assured her. "I didn't know what to tell him either."

"I'm glad I'm not going to go out with him. If I have to go on a first date with someone after twenty years, I'm glad it's you."

The waiter returned with the red wine. They told him they needed a little more time to decide what else they wanted.

"I consent," Pam said to Jess.

"To what?"

"To kiss me if you want to."

Jess pulled her chair around next to Pam and gave her a gentle kiss.

"You're right," Pam said. "It does feel like this is how things should be."

They agreed to make no plans at that moment. They drank wine and watched the boats.

♪♪♪

Jess woke up giddy as a child. She called Aunt Lou. Instead of "Hello," Louanne said, "Tell me everything."

"I feel amazing," Jess said.

"Ha. You alone this morning?"

"Yes."

"Then it couldn't have been that amazing."

"Don't you have any romance in you?"

"Y'all have already had romance," Aunt Lou said. "This friend/romance whatchamadoodle is all I've heard about for a year. The courtship is over. Call me when it gets interesting."

"We watched the boats on the water and held hands."

"That is pretty romantic."

"I told you. I can't wait to see her today. I didn't have this feeling with Alan. Remember when Mom told people she was so proud of me because I wasn't obsessed with him like other teenage girls obsessed with their boyfriends? I just didn't care as much. I feel kind of bad about that."

"He has someone who's obsessed with him now. It all worked out."

"All those stupid love songs are true," Jess said. "If she suddenly went away, I'd die. I'm almost forty. Is that normal?"

"Romantic love doesn't mature past seventeen," Aunt Lou said. "I gotta go. Your mom just walked in."

"Don't tell her anything."

"See," Aunt Lou said. "Love don't mature past seventeen."

Small things changed over the next few days but were somehow huge. When Alex slept over, Pam and Jess would often watch TV together, but this time, they made out before the show was over. Their emojis changed in their text messages. Jess asked a lot of questions.

They sat on a park bench, watching the kids climb a jungle gym. It was hard not to hold Pam's hand or sit close, pressed against her, but they hadn't told the kids anything yet.

"So, what is sex exactly?" she asked Pam.

"Pardon?"

"With women. How do we do that? I feel dumb asking."

"It's a legit question. I mean...you know when it happens."

"I'm afraid I'll be bad at it."

"So am I. It's been years. I'm not worried about you, though. You're a good kisser."

"What's that got to do with it?"

"Your attention to the nuances of kissing shows great promise," Pam said, resting a hand on Jess's thigh.

"You could just show me," Jess said.

"You feel ready for that?"

"I think so."

"It's not the kind of thing you rush," Pam said. "It's okay if you're not."

Jess wasn't. She was thinking too much about it. What didn't help was that her mother showed up at the bakery the next day.

ชะชะชะ

Dreary weather sometimes brought more people into the shop, especially Sundays. Aunt Lou played light jazz or blues just loud enough to hear but not so loud that people had to talk over it. Sometimes, Jess thought of Aunt Lou as a DJ or a party hostess. She knew how to draw people in and make them want to order a second cup of coffee.

"We should set up cots," Jess told Louanne, who was wiping around the coffee pots.

"Shoot, they'd never leave."

Rebecca bolted in from the rain, shaking her umbrella on the floor. She hung it on the coat rack by the door and shivered.

"Au lait with skim," she said, sitting at the bar.

Aunt Lou was already steaming the milk.

"How are you, Mom?" Jess asked.

Rebecca dropped her purse on the counter. "Your dad is having his friends over for the game."

"His regular crew? Mr. Mike?"

"Yes."

"Mr. Paul?"

"Yes."

"Not Uncle Dan."

"He's the number one reason I left the house."

"Don't blame you," Aunt Lou said, setting the au lait on the counter. "Bunch of dude bros."

"Uncle Dan is so loud," Jess said. "Dad is so quiet. How are they brothers?"

"How does he have so many loud friends?" her mom asked. "When your father asked me to marry him, his silence was a big selling point."

"Solid foundation for a marriage," Aunt Lou said.

"Could you see me married to a big talker?"

"Hmm."

"Speaking of marriage," Rebecca said. She sat straighter in her seat and smiled as if speaking of marriage was a better pick me up than the coffee. "Let's talk about getting you a new man."

"Ugh."

"It's like a car. Your old one was a lemon. Let's get you one that really runs. One that can handle the road."

"Mom, how far are you going to take this metaphor?"

"All the way," Aunt Lou said, and snort laughed at herself.

"I'm serious," Rebecca said. "I liked Alan, but he wasn't a family man. What you need is a protector. Someone who's going to make sure that you and the kids get what you need. Maybe a nine-to-five man this time, but one that still makes good money."

"How about a teacher?" Aunt Lou asked.

"No, no," Rebecca said. She wrapped her hands around her mug. "Not enough money."

"But what if this teacher was great," Aunt Lou said. "A gem of a person. One who would always be there for Jess and the kids."

Jess perked up. "And someone who makes me happy. Someone I love, and it wouldn't matter if we don't have a whole lot of money because I wouldn't trade them for anyone."

"It sounds like you have someone in mind," Rebecca said.

"I just," Jess said, "want you to answer the question. Would you be happy if I was happy no matter who it is?"

"No."

"No? Seriously?"

"Well, you seemed like you were happy the first time, and I was happy for you. Look how that turned out. Your brother's marriage seems good. I think Amber is a sweet girl."

"She's a grown woman, not a girl."

"But I'm not going to get attached. These spouses come and go with your generation."

"Um, no. It's the Boomers that started divorcing each other," Jess said.

"Regardless," Rebecca said. "Let's hedge our bets on a good, solid man for you next time around."

Jess would have argued that she didn't really need anybody, but the fact was that she *was* seeing somebody. And that somebody walked through the door at that moment.

Pam pulled back the hood of her raincoat. She beamed at Jess.

Jess was going to have to find a way to tell her mother.

Louanne refreshed her sister's au lait.

Jess untied her apron. "Pam and I are going to grab a sandwich. Want anything?"

"Bring me back a big ole slab of ham," Louanne said.

"Ham sandwich," said Jess, patting Louanne's shoulder. "See you later, Momma."

Jess leaned across the counter to kiss Rebecca on the cheek and left with Pam.

Rebecca stared after her. "I really thought Jess was set, Lou."

"She's doing all right."

"She's getting divorced."

"She's got a job she loves. Two good kids. That's more than most people can say."

"She needs stability. And the kids need a father."

"They have a father."

"Alan? The second he gets that new girl pregnant he'll disappear."

"You might be right. I just don't think you should push her. She's going through a lot."

"That's all the more reason for her to get back out there." Rebecca wrapped her hands around her mug and gave a sly smile. "You know what they say. The best way to get over someone is to get under someone else."

"Rebecca," Louanne said in mock surprise. "Momma's gonna hear you from the grave."

"Who do you think taught me that line?"

"Shut up," Louanne said in genuine surprise.

"Honest to God. Remember the guy I was seeing right before John?"

"No."

"I was devastated when he left me for someone else. Momma told me to stop sniveling and get back out there. That's when I found John."

"And now you got a house full of dude bros hollering at the television."

"I have stability. I want Jess to have that, too." Rebecca shook her head. "I thought I didn't have to worry about her anymore. That she was set for life."

"I guess we don't ever really stop worrying about them."

"It's different. You're her aunt. As a mother, you *want* to stop worrying. Now that Toby has Amber, I can stop worrying that he might be gay."

"Say what?"

"Oh, you remember how I worried about him. He was such a sissy growing up."

Louanne planted both hands on the countertop. "Rebecca. You're an idiot."

"Thanks."

"I don't remember that you worried about Toby. I don't remember who you were with before John because you didn't talk to me until after Momma died. You haven't stopped worrying about Toby because he's with Amber; you just avoid feeling uncomfortable."

"That's not true."

"How much time have you spent with your grandchildren?"

"I saw them last Saturday."

"You saw them when Jess brought them over. When was the last time you went for a walk with them? Played with them?"

"I don't do those things with anybody."

"Maybe you should," Louanne told her. "But you won't because you know Kevin and Betsy are having a hard time and you can't handle it."

"I don't have anything in common with them."

"You don't have anything in common with Jesus either, but you visit Him once a week. Stop trying to get them a new dad and just play Uno with them, for fuck's sake."

"You are not a mother or a grandmother," Rebecca said. "You have no idea."

"Maybe," Louanne allowed. "But I still say that you don't know what your children and your grandchildren really need unless you ask."

Rebecca took a sip of coffee. "It's not true that I always avoid people who make me uncomfortable. *You* still make me uncomfortable."

"Of course, I do. I do it on purpose." Louanne pointed at the mug. "That's whole milk, by the way."

Rebecca pushed the mug away from her as if its mere proximity to her could add fat to her hips.

When Rebecca left, Vivienne stepped out of the kitchen. Louanne slapped the rag over her shoulder and leaned against the counter.

"How can my sister be so ignorant in this day and age?"

"She always has been. You're not going to change her."

"I know." Louanne took her lady's hand and enveloped her in a hug. "You don't have to hide in the back when she's here."

"I wasn't in the mood to pretend that I like her. Or to watch her pretend that she likes me."

Louanne kissed Vivienne's temple. "It's her loss."

5

Kevin knew he was nerdier than the rest of his family, especially his dad's side, but even Aunt Lou didn't seem to get him. He would make a sarcastic remark, and she would look at him strangely, then change the subject. But he knew she liked him because she told him all the time.

"You're a great kid, you know that?" she'd say, out of nowhere, like she'd been thinking about it and made it a point to come tell him.

He didn't understand how she could think he was great when they were so different.

He brought it up to Alex while they were climbing the magnolia tree in his backyard. It was the best climbing tree because it had sturdy branches everywhere he set his feet down, unlike some other trees where the branches were too far apart to climb from one to another. It was so high that, even halfway up, he could see the roof of his house.

"What's it matter if Aunt Lou doesn't get you?" Alex asked, dangling from a limb and letting her feet sway inches from the branch below. "I don't always get you."

"That's true," he said, sitting on the branch above her.

"And she's your aunt, so she's got to like you."

"No, she doesn't. My dad doesn't like me."

Deep down, he had always felt that his father disliked him. But saying it out loud made him burn.

"That's not true," Alex said.

"You should know it's true better than anybody." The burning feeling rose. He didn't like it. "I should have brought a book up here. This would be a nice spot to read."

"Go get some books. We could make a library."

"That's a good idea."

"Bring snacks, too."

"You get the food. I'll get the books."

They scurried down the tree to gather books, notebooks, pens, colored pencils, comics, cookies, water, and oranges. Kevin arranged the books in an old backpack and hung them from a branch. He put the comics and writing materials (should they need them) in Betsy's ladybug backpack, which he stole from her room. Alex had taken all the shoes out of her hanging shoe bag, hung the bag from a thin, strong branch, and put a single-serve snack in each pouch.

"We could live up here," she said.

"I know," Kevin said. "How would we sleep, though?"

"Hammocks?"

"Alex," he said with solemnity. "That is a brilliant idea."

"You think our moms would let us?"

"They've let us camp outside before. This wouldn't be too different."

"Except we'd be off the ground."

He thought about himself suspended, cocooned, and unconscious. "Maybe they wouldn't. And Dad's picking me up soon."

Alex's face fell. "I forgot. We can do it when you come back."

Kevin dug out his copy of *A Wrinkle in Time* from his backpack and leaned back against the tree trunk, his leg dangling off the branch. Alex took a notebook and colored pencils. She began drawing her view of the yard from the tree. They read and drew for a while, and Kevin took a moment to think about how happy he was.

"Let's never come down or go back to school," he said.

"Okay," Alex agreed. She looked up. "We've never been to the top of this tree."

"The branches get too thin up there," Kevin said.

"They get smaller, but I bet they could hold me. I want to see what it looks like. Want to come with me?"

"No."

"Okay," she said. She put the notebook and colored pencils back in the bag and began pulling herself higher into the tree.

Kevin craned his neck to see how far she had to go. "The end of the tree is...pretty up there."

"I know," she said, sounding happy about it.

"What if the branches are too weak for you to stand on?"

"I'll be okay."

"Are you sure you're wearing the proper shoes for this?"

Alex gave him a confused look.

"I'm just concerned," he said.

She set a properly-shoed foot on the next branch up, knocking pieces of loose bark into Kevin's eye.

"Ugh," he said, rubbing his knuckle into his eye socket.

"Son?" his dad called from below. "You ready to go?"

"Um." Kevin blinked against the grit in his wet eyes.

"What are you doing up there?"

"I'm playing football."

"Huh?"

"I said I'm ready."

"I made it!" Alex hollered. She stood on the highest branch she could while holding on to the trunk of the tree. She waved down to Kevin. "Look at me!"

"That's great," said Kevin. "Come down."

"Why didn't you climb up there with her?" his dad asked.

"Because I didn't want to," Kevin said.

"Get on up there and help her."

"I don't need help, Mr. Alan," Alex said, stepping down.

"Don't be silly," his dad said. "Stay there until Kevin can come get you."

"How am I supposed to help her? It's not like I can carry her."

Kevin slipped his book into the bag and climbed down. His dad frowned at him. "I'm disappointed in you, son."

"Why?"

"You should have gone up there with her."

Alex dropped next to him. "He didn't have to."

"Being a man means doing things that you don't always want to do."

Kevin considered the content of his father's "being a man" speeches he'd gotten over the course of his life thus far. According to his dad, being a man meant cleaning his room, helping fix the toilet, lifting furniture, mowing the lawn and, among other things, climbing a tree to help someone who didn't ask for help. By Kevin's assessment, being a man primarily involved doing chores that his dad didn't want to do.

"That doesn't make any sense," Kevin said.

His dad's pale face, which always reddened whenever he stood in the sun for more than a few minutes, reddened deeper.

"Go get your things," he said to Kevin.

Kevin trudged toward the house. His dad huffed alongside him.

"You're punished tonight," his dad told him.

Kevin stopped. "What? Why?"

"For disrespecting me in front of other people."

"Dad-"

"Talking back will only make it worse."

Kevin ran inside the house, away from his dad. He found his mom folding Betsy's clothes into a knapsack.

"Have you seen Betsy's ladybug bag?" she asked. Then she took a good look at him. "What's the matter?"

"I don't want to go to Dad's. Can I stay here?"

"Why?"

He told her what happened. She clasped his hand without saying anything. Then she stepped out of the room, calling for his dad. Kevin snuck into the hall to hear what his mom was telling his dad in the kitchen.

"He's *punished*?" she asked.

"He disrespected me in front of Alex."

"Who cares? Alex is a kid. Kevin only gets to spend four nights with you a month and he's punished?"

"Just for tonight."

"So just one-fourth of the nights he gets to spend with you."

"I wouldn't have to if you were better at setting boundaries," he told her. "Since I moved out, he's gotten a bigger mouth."

"He says what he thinks. I don't find him disrespectful. Not most of the time."

"Oh, you let him get away with everything. You always have."

His dad said his mom was too soft on him and his sister. Exhausted from listening, Kevin went to his bed and tried to read until his dad said it was time to go. His mom gave him and his sister a kiss on the head. She had a smile on her face, but her eyes were red, and there were pink splotches on her cheeks.

"What's the matter?" he asked her.

"Nothing. Be good."

🐦🐦🐦

His dad lived on the second floor of a white brick apartment building. The complex was comprised of four three-story buildings with a swimming pool in the middle of the courtyard. The place was surrounded by a tall, black-barred fence, the kind that slammed behind them with a thunderous rumble.

It was exciting to go there at first. Kevin and Betsy would run to put their duffle bags into the room they shared and would jump into the pool first thing. Kevin had always wanted his own swimming pool. He and his sister would kick around the pool and jump off the diving board while their dad barbequed. That would be the first night. The next day, they would usually go to the park or go shopping, followed by more swimming.

Things had changed a little since he'd gotten together with Cindy. They were still doing the same things, but the activities would be cut short, and it was harder to get his dad's attention. Cindy got into the pool with them now. Betsy liked playing with her, but Kevin felt weird. And since Betsy played with Cindy, Kevin was left to swim around by himself. With Cindy there, it was almost as if his dad felt he didn't need to talk to them or do anything except barbecue and scroll through his phone.

The Friday that Kevin was grounded was even worse. No phone, no computer, and no swimming that night. He would get his stuff back in the morning after a sincere apology. He hoped that the apology didn't involve a confession because he didn't understand what he was apologizing for. He sat in his bed with the door closed, reading his book.

He was at the part in *A Wrinkle in Time* where the kids first cross over into another world to save their dad. He felt a little like Meg Murry—weird, bookish, and missing her father. But in the book, her father had vanished. In Kevin's life, he knew where his dad was. He could walk down the flight of metal stairs to find him flipping burgers by the pool right then if he wanted.

Before the separation, he couldn't remember his dad ever making his mother cry. He couldn't even remember them fighting. He'd only seen his dad angry about understandable things, like the time Kevin spilled a bowl of cereal on his laptop. Since the split, his dad had been perpetually angry. Even when it seemed that he was happy, he could turn suddenly. Kevin never knew when he would get in trouble or understand what he'd done.

The front door opened, and Dad, Cindy, and Betsy's chatter filled the apartment. Kevin smelled hamburger, heard the utensil drawer slide open, and plates clattering on the kitchen table.

Betsy, wet pigtails drooping from the side of her head, stepped inside the room and wiped her nose with the towel draped around her shoulders. How was it that she never got in trouble?

"Dad says to come eat dinner," she said.

"I'm not hungry," he told her.

Betsy yelled through the crack in the door. "Kevin's not hungry!"

"Tell him I say he has to," his dad hollered.

"He says you have to," Betsy reported.

Kevin kept his eyes on his book. "I heard him."

Betsy ran off to relay what he'd said to Dad and Cindy. A minute later, his dad stepped in.

"I didn't say you couldn't eat dinner," he said.

"I know. I'm just not hungry."

"Do you want to be punished again tomorrow?"

"No."

"Then get in there and be polite."

Kevin set down his book and went to the table where Betsy and Cindy sat in their damp bathing suits. Their long, wet hair stuck to their shoulders and smelled like chlorine. The table was in the middle of the huge room, with the kitchen on one end and the living room on the other, so they could watch TV while they ate. His dad kept it on ESPN. A golf tournament was on, and the announcers spoke in hushed voices followed by light clapping. Why anyone would get serious about tapping a ball across grass was beyond Kevin.

During the meal, his dad and Cindy tried a few times to get Kevin to talk, but he gave them one-word answers while he took a few bites from his burger. When Betsy asked if they could watch *Frozen*, Kevin saw his opportunity and asked if he could be excused. His father said he could, but only if he first apologized. "I'm sorry," Kevin said, looking his dad in the face.

His dad reached across the table and laid a hand on his shoulder.

"I'm proud of you," Dad said. "It takes a big man to admit his faults. Next time, you don't question—you just do what I say."

"Got it," said Kevin.

He went back to the room. He wished he could go home and spend the night in the tree with Alex. He hadn't been outside in hours. He didn't want to sit on the couch with Dad, Cindy, and Betsy like they were a family and watch *Frozen* for the hundred thousandth time. He needed to escape. He peeked outside of the bedroom door. Betsy was singing "Let It Go" as loud as she could along with Elsa. Dad and Cindy laughed with her. Kevin snuck to the front door and left the apartment, pulling the door shut slowly behind him.

He wasn't planning to run away. He just wanted to get out of there. He walked along the balcony, running his hand across the iron railing. It felt good to leave and not tell anybody, to walk away from his dad the way his dad had walked away from him so many times. There was the big time when he'd moved out, but there were also times he'd cut conversations short on the phone, or ended their weekend visits a day early because he was tired or needed to spend quality time with Cindy. Walking out of there gave Kevin a charge. It felt good to leave people.

He went down the steps, drawn by the crystal blue pool that glowed from the inside. He took off his shoes and sat on the edge, soaking his feet. Someone had left a pair of brown sandals by the deck chairs. A door opened on the third floor of the building across from him. A man in pajama pants and a T-shirt emerged carrying a bag of garbage.

Then another door opened, and his dad called his name. Kevin ran to the side of the building under the stairwell, directly below Alan. Heavy feet plodded down the stairs, and Kevin scurried along to the side of the building, his heart pumping fast.

"Kevin!"

His dad's voice moved towards him from the other side of the building. Kevin was both angry and pleased that his dad was looking for him. He wanted to be alone, but he wanted to be sought at the same time. He wanted his dad to keep saying his name, fearfully and desperately, as if Kevin was the most important person in the world.

His dad came closer. Kevin ran back into the courtyard and climbed down the ladder into the pool. Climbing down slowly, he didn't make a splash. The water rippled around him, effortlessly making room.

Kevin took a deep breath and plunged underwater when he heard his dad's voice by the pool. He knew he couldn't make himself invisible that way. But he couldn't hear the voice anymore when he was submerged. Everything became still and quiet, except for the bubbles of his breath and the watery echo of his movements when he waved his arms. This was one of those times when he noticed things that had nothing to do with what was happening. He wondered if his arms made a sound when they cut through the air above ground, and he just couldn't hear it. How many things about the world were hidden from him?

There was a splash, and Kevin saw the blur of a man's waist and torso walking through the water. Kevin popped up.

His dad's face was so fierce that Kevin tried to duck under again, but his dad caught him by the back of the shirt and pulled him up.

"What the hell is wrong with you?" Dad screamed.

Both of them were shaking, one with anger, one with fear. Underneath that fear was shame because he had often wondered what *was* wrong with him. He didn't know how to answer that question. He didn't have any words for his dad.

Then two words came to him. "Fuck you!" Kevin hollered as loud as he could.

ᥫᥬ ᥫᥬ ᥫᥬ

Jess had also snuck out of the house. After Alex was tucked into bed, Pam called Jess and told her the door was open. Earlier, when they'd made the plans for the night, Jess had imagined herself trembling with excitement as she hurried down the hall to Pam's bedroom door. In her fantasy, Pam would meet her with an open pajama shirt, breasts, and belly ready to be covered in kisses, and she would take Jess into her arms without a word.

Instead, Jess moped down the hallway, exhausted, her face puffy from crying. She walked into Pam's room and saw the light coming from the master bathroom. Pam appeared with a toothbrush in her mouth.

"Hi," she mumbled. Her honey hair tumbled from a loose bun. She wore a pink cotton T-shirt with pin-striped drawstring pants. "I gotta spit," she said. She ducked back into the bathroom and turned on the tap.

Pam's room was dimly lit by the turquoise lamp on her bedside table. The light gray carpet was freshly vacuumed by the look of the streaks across the floor. It wasn't covered in laundry like Jess's. The white dresser drawers were shut with clothes folded neatly inside them (Jess didn't have to open them to know). The closet door was flush with the wall, not poking open with an avalanche of things spilling out like Jess's. There was a thick, wooden chair next to the dresser, with a bright yellow sun painted on the seat, its orange rays blazing up the back. A black jacket hung from one side of it. The bed looked like it could have been in a furniture advertisement—brass frame, white, puffy comforter, and a line of four plump pillows. It must have been like sleeping on the back of a swan.

How can she like a slob like me? Jess thought.

Pam switched off the bathroom light and pulled the ponytail holder from her hair. It fell wild around her shoulders. The lamplight somehow made it golden and her eyes a brighter shade of green.

"I've brushed my teeth three times," Pam said, sitting on the edge of the bed.

"Why?"

"Dinner was garlicky. I didn't want to kiss you with yucky breath." She patted the bed. Jess sat, and Pam gave her a quick kiss. "How's that?"

Jess smacked her lips. "Minty."

Pam took a good look at her lover's face. "Have you been crying?"

"I got into a fight with Alan. He said I'm not disciplining the kids enough, and then he just started complaining about other things." Jess tried not to cry, which made her start crying all over again. "If I hadn't ended things, Kevin would be okay. And I've screwed up Alan. He used to be a nice guy. What I did made him so angry." Jess rubbed her knuckle against her nose and sniffed. "I'm sorry."

Pam smudged a tear away with her thumb and stroked Jess's temple. "Why are you sorry?"

"Because I wanted to be sexy for you when I came over. Not like this." Jess gestured towards her sobbing, red face.

Pam held her hands, stroking her thumbs over Jess's knuckles. "You can just cry if you need to. We don't have to do anything else."

The permission to simply cry sobered Jess. She stopped crying. Taking away the expectation to fool around made Jess feel light. She'd thought that she would have to bury everything she felt so they could have sex as planned, but Pam was telling her that they didn't have to force it.

"Can I lay down?" Jess asked.

Pam pulled back the covers, and Jess nestled in the soft, swan-feathery bed. Pam snuggled up beside her and took Jess's hand. They lay face to face.

"Thank you," Jess said.

"For what?"

"For letting me be a mess," Jess said. "This can't be fun for you."

"Being a mess is part of the process."

Jess entwined her fingers with Pam's. "But is it worth it? Having to deal with me, and Alan, and the kids..."

Jess was going to keep listing things, but Pam closed her fingers around Jess's and said, "Yes."

Jess buried her face in the crook between Pam's neck and shoulder. Pam gently stroked her back. Jess smelled the clean, lavender soap scent of Pam's skin and kissed her neck. Pam's breath caught, and the feel of the reaction on her lips made Jess kiss her there again. Pam held the back of Jess's head, a soft encouragement to do it again.

"Is this a good spot for you?" Jess asked.

"It drives me crazy," Pam said.

Jess planted small kisses up Pam's long neck, finally reaching her mouth. Pam opened her lips, letting Jess's tongue find hers.

"Breath still good?" Pam asked.

"Mm-hmm," Jess said, rolling on top of her and kissing her again.

Jess felt the rightness of it—being on top of Pam, kissing her deeply, and Pam beginning to rock her hips against Jess's. Jess met her rhythm, mimicking the motion of sex with their clothes on. Jess wanted nothing more but to feel inside of Pam, to see if she would react the same way as she did to Jess's kiss on her neck.

Jess slid her hand underneath the band of Pam's pajama pants. Her hip was soft and warm. Jess pulled her pants down a little and kissed her hip and the place below her belly button. Pam moaned. She began to pull her pants further down—then realized what she was doing.

Jess froze. "Oh, I'm...I'm about to...I don't know how to do that."

Pam propped up on her elbows. "You don't have to."

"But I want to," Jess told her. "I'm just afraid I won't make you feel good."

"It's okay," Pam said. "I've got the map."

She took Jess's hand, and guided it into her underwear. Jess's felt the brush of Pam's hair under her fingertips, and then touched flesh. It was warm and wet on the pad of the forefinger. Jess spread the wetness along the ridge of Pam's lips, marveling at the feel of them. Jess had the impulse to suck on them, but she was afraid she wouldn't do it right, so she kept stroking them. Pam pulled her legs apart, inviting Jess's hand inside of her, but they were caught by her pants. Jess pulled the pants all the way down and threw them on the floor. Then she sat back on her knees, beholding all six feet of the woman before her.

Pam sat up and scooted across the bed, leaning alongside Jess. Jess shifted her legs, sitting on the mattress and cradling Pam. Pam's knees fell open. She took Jess's hand, leading it back to her slit, and pulled her fingers inside of her. Jess's two fingers sheathed into a space that was soft, tight, excited, and alive.

Pam moaned into Jess's mouth, leading her fingers to a certain spot that felt hard, like there was bone underneath. Jess pushed against the spot and Pam made a sound that was a cross between pleasure and pain. She took her hand away and let Jess explore the spot on her own. She grasped Jess's shoulder and bucked her hips against Jess's hand.

Jess then asked a question that she already knew the answer to, but wanted reassurance.

"Is this it?" Jess asked. "Is this sex?"

"Yes," Pam said, laughing. "Keep doing what you're doing."

Jess kept stroking that one spot, Pam panting harder and biting Jess's shirt to keep from screaming. The space around Jess's fingers tightened and a rush of fluid washed over them. Pam moaned and suddenly relaxed. Jess stopped moving.

"Did I just make you cum?" she asked.

Pam nodded. "You're good at instructions."

Jess drew her fingers out slowly and pulled Pam's shirt off.

"Tell me what to do now," Jess said.

An hour later, Jess's phone rang. Jess almost missed the call. She and Pam were still exploring each other's bodies, and discovering what felt good to the other.

It hadn't even felt like an hour. From the moment that Jess had slid her fingers inside of Pam, and they kissed and moved against each other, Jess understood what sex was supposed to feel like. It was the connection that she'd always heard about but never felt before. It changed the definition of what sex was. She'd been taught that it was only officially happening when a penis was inside a vagina, but it turned out that was only one way to do it. This, *this* was also sex. She wanted it to keep going on and on. And it could have, except that she'd left her phone on in case there was an emergency with the kids, and Alan was calling.

Jess answered in a confused, sleepy voice. Her skin was hot and red, her heart was beating fast, and her head was drunk with sex.

"What in the hell is going on with Kevin?" Alan growled.

"Why, what's wrong?" she asked.

Alan told her the story of Kevin sneaking out of the apartment and hiding in the pool with his clothes on.

"Can I talk to him?" Jess asked.

Pam sat up next to Jess and switched on her bedside lamp.

"I made him go to bed," Alan said. "Is something going on at home that I don't know about?"

"No. It sounds like he was just angry and hiding from you."

"Don't make this about me. What is wrong with that kid?"

Jess's guilt from earlier was fading. Maybe it was the orgasms that grounded her.

"Nothing is *wrong* with him," she said. "He's going through a hard time."

"Betsy's going through a hard time too, but she's not crazy."

"Kevin isn't crazy. I have to go."

"Don't get off the phone with me. We need to talk about this."

"Yelling at me isn't going to fix anything," she said.

"You need to come get him."

"You said he's sleeping."

"He's having a crisis, and you're not going to come get him?"

"He's not having a crisis right now. He's in bed and I'm with Pam."

"When he wakes up, I'll tell him that drinking with a buddy was more important to his mother than taking care of him."

"Alan," Jess said. "When the kids are with you, at bare minimum, you need to keep them from sneaking out of your apartment and drowning."

"I-"

"Can you keep Kevin alive until morning?"

"I'm sure as shit going to have to keep an eye on him now."

"Good. I have to open the shop tomorrow, but you can bring him to me."

"He can bring him here," Pam told her.

"Oh," Jess said. "Bring him to Pam."

Jess set the phone down. She closed her eyes and rubbed her forehead with her fingers.

Pam draped the blanket across Jess's shoulders and took her hand.

"Do you think I did the right thing?" Jess asked her.

"Yeah. I think it would be more chaotic for Kevin to pick him up in the middle of the night."

"But we have a date tomorrow," Jess lamented. "I'm sorry."

"Aunt Lou is going to watch Alex for me. Maybe she can watch Kevin and Betsy too."

Pam sat back against the headboard and opened her arms so Jess could lie on her chest. She kissed Jess's head. "When we get the kids back tomorrow, can we call Alan and complain while he's having sex?"

"Yes."

୬୬ ୬୬ ୬୬

"That dick brain," Louanne said after Jess told her about Alan's phone call. "Are the kids back home?"

Jess nodded. "He's dropping them off to Pam in a little while. Kevin called me at 5:00 this morning and asked to come home. He said he couldn't sleep last night. Betsy wants to stay with Alan, but he told her she had to come home too."

"I'll take them to do something fun tonight."

"Thank you."

"Want to come with, Sugar?" Louanne asked Vivienne.

"I've got book club tonight," Vivienne answered from the kitchen.

"That's right," she said, with a sigh. "I can never keep up with your meeting schedule."

"It's been the first Saturday of every month for five years," Vivienne said.

Louanne leaned against the wall and sighed. She wasn't sure what would cheer up Kevin. He was harder for Louanne to bond with than Jess had been. With Jess, it had been easy. She could take her camping or bake cupcakes with her.

It shouldn't have surprised her that mother and son were so different. Louanne had grown up feeling alien from her own mother and father. If she didn't have her father's sideways smile and her mom's hips and hands, she would have thought she was adopted. Instead, she was a Frankenstein of their features, and in her head was a brain from outer space.

That evening was cool and clear. Louanne would have loved to ride her motorcycle, but riding over in the light meant riding back in the dark, and her night vision had gotten worse in the last couple of years. When she was younger, she would have ridden over to Jess's house blindfolded just to see if she could do it. Now, everything had death creeping around the corner for everybody. The fear made her feel old. Was youth, she wondered, the absence of fear?

"Nope," she thought, listening to Kevin explain why he wasn't skating in the driveway with Alex and Betsy.

"I don't like to go fast," Kevin said.

Every time Alex sped up and twisted right before she hit the road, he'd hold his breath. His whole body tensed. So, youth had nothing to do with the absence of fear. Kevin was the same age as Alex, yet they were so different. Alex wanted to hop into the road. Kevin trembled at the sight of those spinning wheels like they could run him over.

"You just gonna stand there watching them?" she asked Kevin.

"I don't mind," he said, clutching the book in his hands.

"What are you reading?" she asked.

"*A Wrinkle in Time,*" he said. "I have to read it for school. But it's good."

"School's a whole month away. You're getting the jump on it, huh?"

"Reading is the only part of school I like. Did you like school?"

Louanne shrugged. "Not particularly. I didn't want to learn anything, and I was a girl who looked like a boy. It was an all-around fail."

Kevin smiled.

"You got your great-grandfather's sideways smile," she said. "Anyone ever tell you that?"

"No."

"I got it, too," she gave her best imitation of her father's smile as a demonstration. "Tell me about that book."

Kevin flipped through the paperback, describing it. He did so with the care of a much older man touching delicate pages.

"Aunt Lou, watch me," Betsy said.

The six-year-old coasted along and then stopped where the driveway met the road.

"Betsy," Kevin said. "You're too close to the road."

"You're not the boss of me, Kevin."

"I'm the boss of you," Louanne said. "Don't get so close to the road."

"It's Kevin's fault we're not at Dad's house," Betsy said. She'd said it as a matter of fact with a snide tone.

"No, it's not," Louanne corrected her. "That was your dad's decision."

"He decided it because Kevin ran away."

"Go skate and stay out of the road."

"Can I go in the road?" Alex asked Louanne.

Alex stood at the edge of it, one skate rolling back and forth in quick jerks, ready to launch.

"Not right now," said Louanne.

"But this is boring," she complained.

"It is," Louanne agreed.

She'd been standing up all day at the bakery. Her hips and lower back hurt standing in that driveway watching the kids.

"Let's go see a movie," she said.

"Which one?" Kevin asked.

"'Guardians of the Galaxy' is supposed to be good."

Kevin nodded approval. Alex hopped on her skates in delight. Betsy seemed skeptical.

"Three against one, Betsy," Louanne told her. "Go get shoes on. We'll hit the arcade first."

Louanne had made this decision thinking that Jess and Pam were going to dinner, but they had also decided to see a movie. Kevin saw them before everyone else. His mom and Miss Pam were in the ticket line. They were holding hands, which didn't strike him as odd. Sometimes girls did that. But then Miss Pam wrapped her arms around his mom, kissed the top of her head, and they swayed together as if to music. Kevin had never seen his parents hold each other like that, or his dad and Cindy for that matter.

"Momma!" Betsy cried, and the women separated.

"I'm sorry, y'all," Louanne told them. "They were getting restless, so I thought I'd take them out."

Jess hefted Betsy to her hip and kissed her cheek. Pam mussed Alex's hair.

"All right, y'all," Louanne said. "If we don't hit the Game Room now, we won't have time to play before the movie starts."

She shooed them into the theater and headed for the Game Room. Kevin looked back at the women. They had returned to their embrace.

Alex was looking back, too. "Finally," she said.

Kevin stopped walking. "Finally, what?"

"I was wondering when they'd get together."

"They're not *together*."

"Hey, slow pokes," Louanne called. She stood outside the flashing lights of the arcade. Betsy was already lost inside of it.

Kevin ran to her. "Alex says Mom and Miss Pam are girlfriends."

Louanne's expression didn't change the way Kevin thought it would.

"What makes you think that?" Louanne asked Alex.

"My mom's gay," Alex said.

"That's not a reason," Louanne said. "I'm gay. I don't find most women attractive. What makes you think they want to be girlfriends?"

"They act like they are."

"Hmm," said Louanne. "You should ask them."

"Can't you just tell us?" Kevin asked.

"No," she said. She held up two quarters. "I want to kick someone's butt at air hockey."

"Me," Alex said. She hurried over to the air hockey table.

"Doesn't this bother you?" Kevin asked Alex.

"No. Mom's always been gay."

"My mom's not."

"She is now."

Kevin wandered around the arcade, watching other kids zap spaceships, beat the stuffing out of each other, and drive pixelated cars at insane speeds. He felt detached from all of it.

Louanne's hand came down on his shoulder. "What's the matter, Chief?"

"Everything's changing."

"I know."

"I want to go home."

"The movie's gonna start soon," she said. "I really think you should talk to your mom when she gets home."

Kevin, who no longer wanted to be in the same building with anyone in his family, stopped talking.

The movie had superheroes who wouldn't stop talking. They were supposed to be funny. This guy beat up villains and saved people with constant chatter that most of the audience found hilarious. It only made Kevin hate him more because he would have to open his mouth to laugh. He would have to lighten the heaviness, but he didn't want to. The characters were all happy little idiots, beating up people and joking about it. Everyone was such an idiot.

He didn't talk on the ride home, and went to bed before his mom got back. He was awake when he heard her walk in. He squeezed his eyes shut when she opened the door.

"Kevin?" she asked, timidly.

He heard her footsteps across the floor and felt the sink of weight next to him. His mom sighed and softly petted his hair. When she left, he was able to fall asleep.

He woke up to someone else tapping his face.

"Kevin," Alex whispered. "Kevin, Kevin, Kevin, Kevin-"

"I'm awake." He brushed her hand away. "Stop."

"Ha!" she said, triumphantly. "You're talking."

He snapped on his lamp and leaned against the wall, drawing his covers up to his pajama shirt. Alex was still fully dressed, as if she'd been too excited to get ready for bed.

"What time is it?" he asked.

"I don't know. Listen. Our moms *are* together."

"How do you know?"

"I asked them," she said. "After you and Betsy went to bed."

Kevin got out of bed and started pacing, feeling like a shaken-up soda can.

"I was thinking," Alex said, crossing her legs. "Our moms should get married."

"Married? Can they do that?"

"I don't know. But they should. They're so cute together! Think about it. I mean, if they're both gonna be gay, why not? We could be a real family. Your mom even hugs me like a real mom. You and me could be brother and sister! We could live together!"

Kevin looked at his old soccer ball on the floor and kicked it against the wall.

"Are you mad?" Alex asked.

"Yes! Why aren't *you* mad?"

"Because we could be a family."

"I had a family! Why do my parents have to be with other people at all?"

"Don't you want them to be?"

"No."

"Don't you want to be my real brother?"

Kevin stopped pacing. The room felt too small. "I don't know. I need to go outside."

He sat next to her and put his tennis shoes on.

"It's nighttime," she told him.

Kevin opened up his window and took the screen down.

"What are you doing?"

"I want to get out," Kevin stopped with one leg raised up on the windowsill. "My dad is probably going to marry Cindy. Then I'll have three moms. I'm already weird enough, Alex."

"Kevin."

He climbed out the window.

"Wait for me," she said, scrambling after him.

Kevin sprinted towards the street as soon as his feet hit the ground.

"Kevin!" Alex called behind him.

He couldn't slow down. His body told him to speed up, to burn off the bubbling feeling inside of him. He heard Alex's voice, but it was distant, and the part of him that didn't want to hurt her was closed off from the animal that had taken over and needed to move, needed to feel his muscles and his lungs burn.

But Alex was faster. Barefoot, she ran past him, the loud pink of her tank top shouting in front of him in the dark. He had a burst of competitive energy, and for a few seconds, they were neck and neck, but he fell back and she shot further ahead. Frustrated and spent, he slowed until he came to a halt by the stop sign on the corner. Alex was still going without looking back.

"You win," he wheezed.

Her feet slowed, and her run became a jog. Then she stopped, breathing heavily, and looked over her shoulder at him. He bent forward, holding onto his knees, grateful for the exhaustion that numbed out feeling. He looked up at the sound of quick feet coming at him.

Alex stopped in front of him, fists tight against her sides.

"You can run away from your mom and dad," she spat through her teeth. "But you can't run away from me. Who would I have if you left? It would just be me and Mom again and we're not enough!"

Kevin tried to catch his breath. "I wasn't running from you."

"Yes, you were! And you can't! I'm faster than you! Don't ever think you can outrun me. I'm the fastest human being that ever lived! Do you believe me?"

"Yes, I believe you."

"Why don't you want me to be your sister?"

"I do—stop yelling," he said, using the trick he learned from his mom of lowering his voice so that she would lower hers.

"No!" she cried, opening her hands and planting her feet solidly in the street. "No, I won't! Don't complain about three moms and a dad! I don't even know my dad! You think I've never wanted a normal family? You're not the only one who wants that, Kevin!"

Kevin looked around to see if anyone was listening to them. They were alone, but he was still nervous.

"Okay, okay," he said. "I'm sorry. Can you stop yelling? You're going to wake people up."

"I'm not the one who decided to run down the street in the middle of the night. Tell me why you don't want me to be your sister."

"Because..."

"Because why!"

"Because what if we want to get married someday?"

She stopped yelling and stared at him.

"Do you like me?" she asked.

He made a disgusted face. "No."

"Then why would you want to marry me?"

"Well, we'll marry somebody, won't we? I just thought it might be nice."

"So, you weren't running from me?"

"No. I just wanted to run." Something clicked in Kevin's brain. "Maybe our moms are together because they're friends like us."

"You think?"

"They're best friends."

She shrugged. "Maybe that's true for your mom. My mom's hella gay."

They walked back down the street towards their houses. Kevin listened to the cicadas.

"Will people make fun of us?" he asked.

"No," Alex said. "Juan Pedro and Desmond in my class have two moms. And Courtney in fifth, has two dads."

"That's true. They look gayer than our moms, though. Our moms don't really look gay, do they?"

"It's mean to talk like that," Alex told him.

"But it's true," Kevin insisted.

"Well, it doesn't matter; they are and they love each other so they should get married. I could have a brother and a sister."

"I do like your mom more than I like Cindy," Kevin admitted.

"What's your problem with Cindy?"

Kevin shrugged. "She's boring."

"You can be boring too. Tonight, when you weren't talking, that was boring."

"I'm sorry."

Alex hugged him suddenly and tightly. He forgot what to do with his arms, so he allowed himself to be hugged.

"Don't run away again," she said.

"I won't if you don't want me to," he said.

6

Jess woke up to Betsy singing "Let it Go" to herself in her bedroom. Jess imagined Betsy flinging her arms wide open, doing her best Elsa imitation as she sang.

Jess felt none of the easy freedom of "Let It Go." She felt more like "Stay in Bed." If that wasn't a Disney song, it should have been. So, she pulled the covers over her head and sang words that felt more appropriate to her situation.

"Stay in bed," she sang to herself, with all the gusto of a winded old woman. "Stay in bed. Don't let the covers come off of your head. Todaaaaaaay, they will all know you're gay. Stay in bed. Stay in bed."

She snatched her phone from the bedside table and brought it under the blanket to call Pam.

"I wrote a song for you," she told Pam. "Want to hear it?"

"Sure." After Jess sang, Pam said, "From now on, just bring me flowers."

"You didn't like my song?"

"I did. I thought it was cute and sad. Are you really hiding in bed?"

"Yeah. Aren't you?"

"No. Alex and I are eating waffles and watching cartoons."

"Hi, Miss Jess!" Alex hollered in the background. She yelled something else that Jess didn't understand.

"Did you hear that?" Pam asked.

"No."

"She wants us to get married."

Jess flung the blanket off her face. "Ha! I guess she's still okay with it then."

When they told Alex the night before, Jess was afraid that Alex was pretending to be happy for their sake. She was a nice kid. That seemed like something Alex might have done.

Or maybe she was in shock and the feelings hadn't been processed yet.

"I think she's processing just fine," Pam said when Jess voiced her concerns. "She wants to be our flower girl."

"Did you tell her it isn't legal?"

"She doesn't think in those terms. I've dragged her to a lot of commitment ceremonies. You haven't talked to Kevin and Betsy yet?"

"No, you're the first person I've talked to." Jess thought about Alex tossing flower petals down a long, white path with Jess and Pam following her towards an altar. "I like it when you're the first person I talk to in the morning."

"Me too," Pam said. "Just to warn you, Kevin knows. Alex told him last night."

She sat up. "How did he take it?"

"She said he was upset at first, but she calmed him down."

"I love that girl."

"She's the best."

Jess gathered her resolve. "Okay. I need to get up and go have a talk with them."

What does one wear, she thought, when one comes out to her children? And how exactly was she coming out to them? As someone who was in a relationship with Pam? Someone who was queer in general? Or both? She didn't have doubts about whether or not she was a lesbian anymore. Louanne had been right. She had to have sex with a woman to know. In fact, she hadn't even needed to go that far. Even kissing was a different experience. She knew through her core that she didn't want to have sex with men. Even if she wasn't with Pam, she wouldn't be with a man again.

For that conversation, she decided that she needed to wear something that said, "I'm still your mom." She plucked a bra from the floor by her bed. She'd only worn it the last two days, so it was relatively clean. Black gym shorts and a purple LSU basketball T-shirt.

Both kids were still in their rooms. She put the coffee on and took eggs and blueberries from the refrigerator. She needed to do something normal, and thought that brewing coffee and pulling something out of the oven would calm her. She played Mazzy Star and cracked eggs into a silver bowl.

Kevin shuffled his slippered feet into the kitchen. His paperback hung loose in his hand, the way he used to carry around a teddy bear.

"Hey, Mom," he said.

"Hey, kiddo," she told him.

She added milk, oil, and vanilla and began to whisk. She felt his eyes on her. He stood in front of the refrigerator without moving or speaking.

She set down the whisk. "I know Alex told you about me and Miss Pam's conversation last night."

He nodded.

"Do you have any questions for me?"

"Is it true?" he asked. "Miss Pam's your girlfriend?"

"Yes."

"Why?"

"Because we fell in love."

He sat at the kitchen table. "So, are you gay?"

"Yes," she said.

It almost surprised her to say it with such certainty.

"Why weren't you gay before?"

"What do you mean?"

"You were with Dad. So, did you turn gay?"

"No," Jess said. "I think I was before. I just didn't know myself and had only ever dated your dad. I was scared, too. It wasn't as acceptable when I was a kid as it is now."

"Did you lie to Dad?"

Jess thought about how she felt when she met Alan. A skinny sixteen-year-old boy in swim trunks at the community pool she and Toby went to. Alan didn't come on to her like other guys. He just talked about things and asked her about herself. He was nice to Toby, and she had a soft spot for anyone who was kind to her small, shy brother. Alan had been so nervous to ask her out that his friend had to ask her for him. She found him intelligent and endearing. Her love for him hadn't been a lie.

"No, I didn't lie to Dad. I think that's why he's confused."

"It is confusing," Kevin said. "How would you not know?"

"It's kind of hard to explain."

"Does that mean that I could be gay and not know it? Like, I could suddenly change?"

Jess laid a hand on his. "No. You're a completely different person. It was hard for me to face."

"It would be hard for me to face too," he said. "Dad already thinks I'm weird."

"If you were," Jess told him, "your dad would still love you."

"How do you know that? He doesn't even want me around now. Does Dad know about you?"

"Not yet. I'm going to tell him now that you know. And Betsy, too."

"You're not going to leave, are you?"

"Kevin," she said. "No. I might not have known who I wanted to be with when I was younger, but I've always wanted to be your mom."

"You didn't know I'd be your kid."

"Well, I always wanted kids. If I had met Miss Pam before I met your dad, I still would have wanted to have you. You're smart and funny. And handsome and interesting."

Kevin's lip trembled. "Why doesn't Dad like me?"

Jess put an arm around him. "Your dad's just angry right now, honey. It's not you. If anyone, he's mad at me."

"He hates me," Kevin said.

"No, he doesn't. He's just being dumb."

"He is dumb," Kevin said. "Please don't tell him I cried."

"I won't," she said.

"Are you making blueberry muffins?"

"Uh-huh."

"Can I put the blueberries in?"

That was his last question of the morning. He dumped the blueberries into the mixing bowl and spooned the batter into the muffin pan.

Betsy appeared while Kevin sprinkled brown sugar crumbles on top of the uncooked muffins.

"What are you doing?" Betsy asked.

"Mom's gay," Kevin said.

"Kevin," Jess said. It was not how she wanted Betsy to find out.

"No, she's not," Betsy said.

"Yeah, she is, and Miss Pam's her girlfriend," Kevin said.

"How do you know?"

"She told me."

"Is that true, Momma?" Betsy asked.

"Yes."

"Oh," Betsy said. She pointed to the mixing bowl on the counter. "Can I lick the bowl?"

Jess passed it to her with a spoon. Betsy carried her prize into the living room and sat in front of the television. Phineas and Ferb were building something impossible in their backyard.

In Jess's eyes, the biggest difference between Kevin and Betsy was that Kevin felt everything. Betsy was okay with any situation as long as she could slap on a tiara and sing. But watching her daughter immediately escape into muffin batter and cartoons made her wonder if her children were all that different. Was it that Kevin felt more and Betsy felt less? Or did they just deal with it differently?

Jess stepped into the living room and Kevin followed.

"Are you okay, Betsy?" Jess asked.

"Uh-huh."

"You can talk to me if you want to ask me anything or tell me something," Jess said.

"Okay," she said, eyes fixed on the television.

"You're not going to kiss in front of us, are you?" Kevin asked.

"Ew," Betsy said.

"Probably not today."

"Can Miss Pam and Alex come over?" Kevin asked. "Can I go get them?"

"Yes, you can," Jess said.

Just as Jess pulled the muffins from the oven, Pam and Alex walked through the kitchen door. They ate while Kevin and Alex asked them question after question. It was easier for Jess to answer with Pam next to her, holding her hand under the table.

After a while, Betsy came into the kitchen with a muffin batter mustache. She put the bowl on the counter. "Can I call Dad?"

Jess didn't want her to. She'd wanted to come out to Alan personally, but asking Betsy not to talk about it felt wrong. Betsy, Jess thought, should be able to talk about it to her dad. Not talking about things had been a problem in her family for too long.

"Um," Jess said. "Sure. And wipe your face."

Betsy ran her tongue across her upper lip and ducked back into the living room. A few minutes later she was back, holding the phone to Jess.

"He wants to talk to you," she said.

Jess glanced at Pam who looked back at her like she wanted to catch Jess from falling off a cliff. Jess accepted the phone, and no sooner was the phone at her ear when Alan said, "You're fucking the neighbor?"

"I'm going to talk to him outside," Jess said. When she was securely in the backyard she said, "I'm seeing Pam."

"Did she come on to you?"

"No. We just started to have feelings for each other."

"She always checked you out."

"It's not all her," Jess said. "I think I'm more of a lesbian."

"More of a lesbian than what?"

"Than a straight person."

"No, you're not."

"Think about it, Alan."

In the silence that followed, she knew that both of them were thinking about the sex life they'd shared for twenty years.

"Were you gay that whole time?" he asked.

"I think so, yeah."

"Did you cheat on me?"

"No."

"Why didn't you tell me?"

"I guess I just didn't let myself think about it."

"Well thanks," he said. "Thanks a lot."

He hung up.

Later that day he knocked on the door. Betsy shrieked with joy at the sight of him. Kevin laid low in his room.

"Hey honey," he said to Betsy. "I need to talk to your mom alone for a minute."

They went into the backyard and sat on the swing. Jess stirred the dirt with the tip of her tennis shoe.

"Do you think that Kevin's gay?" Alan asked.

Kevin glided past the bay window in the kitchen, book in front of his face.

"No," she said. "Why?"

"Look at him."

"Reading doesn't make him queer."

"He reminds me of your brother," Alan said. "He's sensitive like him."

"Toby's bi," Jess allowed. "But there are straight sensitive men, you know. Anyway, would it be so bad if he was?"

"It's not that it would be bad," Alan said. "I just already don't understand him. How much more different from me is he going to become? He doesn't even look like me. He looks like a clone of you. Betsy is the only one I see myself in. I didn't see that coming."

"He just wants you to be with him," Jess said. "Let him show you who he is."

"I don't know what I'm doing," Alan said.

"With what?"

"This parenting thing. You always did it. You knew what to say, when to punish them, when to let things go. I don't know what I'm doing. I don't even know when they're sick. Does a cold make them officially sick and they need to stay in bed, or is it not a big deal and they need to suck it up?"

"It just depends."

"Depends on what?"

"It's a case-by-case basis kind of thing. I don't always know what I'm doing either."

"You look like you do," Alan said. "I just keep fucking everything up."

"That's not true."

"Kevin ran away and hid in a pool."

"He's just mad," she said. "Confused."

"What do we do about that?"

"Shit, Alan," Jess said. "I just blew his mind by coming out. How would I know?"

"Why are there so many gay people in your family?"

"They say it's genetic."

"And there was no point in the time we were together that you thought you might be? We were together ten years before we got married."

"There was a lot of incentive to ignore it," Jess said. "And I loved you."

"That's just more confusing," Alan told her.

"I know," Jess said.

They rocked gently in the swing.

"Is there anything else you need to tell me?"

"No."

"I would have let you sleep with women if I'd known that's what you wanted. We could have opened up our relationship."

"I wouldn't have wanted that," Jess said.

"You could have tried," Alan said. "It didn't feel like you tried. It felt like one day you were happy and the next day you wanted a divorce."

"Mm-hmm." Jess vigorously nodded her head. "I'm sure it did seem that way from your perspective."

"What's that supposed to mean?"

"It was the same with me as it is with Kevin. You need to listen to people when they talk to you. I didn't say 'I'm a lesbian,' but I told you that I was unhappy."

"No, you didn't. When did you say you were unhappy?"

"So many times."

"Kevin hasn't said he's unhappy," Alan said.

"He's not going to say it directly like I did. Spend some time with him without telling him what to do. Let him talk."

"I'm the dad. He's supposed to listen to me."

"I'm not saying that you have to let him be in charge. Just get to know him without trying to control who he is."

"Maybe." Alan leaned back and folded his arms. "I tried to make you happy."

"I know you did."

"I didn't want to divorce you," he said.

"I'm sorry I hurt you, Alan. I really am."

"You say that like it's something you couldn't help."

"I think this is one of those things that I can't control," she said. "I tried, and it caught up with me with a vengeance."

"So, it's not just me?" Alan said. "It's all men you don't want to be with?"

"Yeah, it's not you."

Alan nodded, taking it in. "I wish you would have told me before Betsy did."

"I planned to, but word traveled fast."

"Does Rebecca know yet?"

"No."

"You might want to tell her before Betsy blurts it out over the phone."

"I'm sorry," Jess said. "I didn't mean for—"

"For it to mess up my whole life?" Alan said.

"Yes."

"Is," Alan said. "Is she good to you?"

The question took her a moment to answer, not because she doubted that Pam was wonderful—she was just surprised he asked it.

"She is," Jess said.

"Good."

Alan went into the house to say his goodbyes to the kids. Jess stayed on the swing for a long time after he left.

♊♊♊

The next day was Monday, which meant there was a good bit of downtime after the morning rush. Jess leaned against the counter next to Louanne and assumed her pose—arms folded, staring into nothing.

"So," Jess said, breaking Louanne's trance. "I told Alan and the kids about me and Pam."

"How did it go?"

"Umm," Jess said.

There were too many answers to that question. Alan, Kevin, and Betsy were all confused, weirded out, hurt, and hopeful, and Jess felt all of those things too.

"That good, huh?" Louanne said.

"It didn't go horribly. I feel like I disappointed them all somehow. Like I betrayed them."

"Why do you say that?"

"They all thought of me as one person, and now I'm another."

"No, you're not."

"They don't know that," Jess said.

"This is what's happening," Vivienne called from the kitchen. "Their idea of who you are is butting up against their idea of what a lesbian is."

Jess and Louanne looked back at her in the kitchen doorway. Vivienne was piping yellow flowers onto a chocolate cake.

"The kids have known you and me as a couple all their lives," Louanne said. "They should be more familiar with lesbians than most."

"We're not their mom, though. Kids don't like it when the idea of who their momma is gets upended. We've had friends come out late. We've seen it before." Vivienne stopped piping for a moment and looked at Jess. "It's going to be all right. After a while, they'll see you're still the same person."

"At least it won't be like me coming out to your mother," Louanne said.

The bell stopped the conversation. Toby came in, cradling a puppy. It was an infant basset hound with ears that draped over Toby's arm. Its skin sagged over its eyes, making it look sleepy.

"I want to introduce you guys to someone," Toby sang, wiggling the puppy's paw.

Jess rushed out from behind the counter and took the warm puppy. It grunted and licked her face. Louanne followed her, making the same kind of cooing noises as Jess, but said, "Look how adorable. Toby, get it out of my bakery."

"No," Jess said, hugging the puppy to her.

"You've got to start letting dogs in, Aunt Lou," Toby told her. "All the coffee shops are cool with dogs. You'd get more foot traffic."

"And poop," said Louanne.

"What's its name?"

"Her name is Louanne after the best aunt in the whole wide world," Toby said.

Louanne leveled her eyes with his.

"Her name is Pepper," he said.

Jess smashed her face into the puppy's side and muttered about how adorable it was.

"I guess she needs an emotional support dog right now," Louanne said.

"How come?" Toby asked.

"I came out to the kids," Jess told him.

She told him how it went.

"If you're not busy today," Jess said, "could you bring this little one over to Pam and the kids? They could use puppy therapy too."

"Sure," he said. "Have you told Mom yet?"

"No. But she'll be in soon for her usual."

"Hmm. Make my coffee to-go."

"Coward," Jess said, passing the hound back to him.

"Yes, I am," he admitted.

Jess walked back behind the counter with Louanne and washed her hands at the sink.

"Did you ever tell mom you've dated guys?" she asked.

"Hell no," he said. "I don't tell Mom and Dad anything about my life. But I didn't fall in love with anyone until I met Amber. If I'd had something with a man like I have with her, I would have told Mom. You think that's what you have?"

"Yeah," Jess said.

Toby smiled. "Pretty great, isn't it?"

Louanne set Toby's coffee on the counter. "Would you please take your love and puppies out of here?"

The bell rang on the door. Rebecca sang hello before she was completely inside and waved to Toby, ignoring the rest of them, her gold bracelets sliding down her slender wrist halfway to her elbow. Her light pink nails matched her light pink lipstick. With her white sun dress, white patent leather purse with the gold chain on her shoulder, and cotton candy sandals, Jess thought she looked like an Easter egg.

Rebecca went to embrace Toby, but then she stopped, her smile sliding into a scowl.

"Son," she said. "You can't bring a dog in here. It's unsanitary."

"Exactly," Louanne said.

Rebecca took a chair at the counter. "When are you and Amber going to have human babies?"

"This is it," Toby said, presenting Pepper. "This is the only kind of baby we want."

"How do Amber's parents feel about that?" Rebecca asked.

"They don't think we should have children if we know we don't want them."

Rebecca rolled her eyes. "Of course, they think that. They're hippies. What's the point of marriage if not to have children?"

Toby and Jess exchanged glances.

"What?" Rebecca asked.

Louanne set a skinny latte in front of her sister. "Is that why you married John? Easy access sperm donor?"

"Don't be crass," Rebecca said.

"Pepper is your granddog, Mom," Toby said. He shuffled Pepper in his arms so he could take his coffee with his free hand. He kissed Rebecca on the cheek. "Love her as you love me." Turning to Jess, he said, "I'll take her over to meet the kids before I go home."

Louanne asked him if he wanted a muffin to go with his coffee. He said no, but before he could get away, Louanne pulled a gingersnap out of her apron and fed it to Pepper.

"Lou," Toby whined.

"It's not gonna hurt her," she said, scratching the dog's chin as it chewed. "I make them myself."

"Do you keep cookies in your apron all the time?"

"Why are you judging me? You want me to welcome this little turd back here or not?"

"You said she was unsanitary."

"Well," Louanne said, scratching Pepper behind a huge ear. "That was before I realized she was my niece."

Pepper gave her aunt grateful kisses all over her nose.

Toby left, and Jess stared at her mother, knowing what she had to do.

"Aunt Lou, can I take a fifteen? I want to have coffee with my mom."

Rebecca set down her mug. "You do?"

Jess took off her apron and poured herself a cup of medium roast, forgetting the cream and sugar. She guided Rebecca to a table near the back. The shop was always empty this time of the day, but she wanted to make sure they weren't interrupted by customers. The only sound was Bessie Smith playing over the speakers.

Jess wrapped her hands around her coffee mug.

"What do you want to tell me?" Rebecca asked. It was more of a statement than a question. Her tone suggested that whatever Jess had to say, she was already disappointed.

"How do you know I want to tell you something?" Jess asked.

"Because you look guilty."

"I'm not guilty," Jess said, sipping coffee.

"Yes, you are."

"I have nothing to feel guilty about. I haven't done anything wrong."

"So, you're superhuman with no capacity for wrongdoing?"

"I didn't say that."

"Even Jesus sinned," Rebecca reminded her.

"Mom." Jess rubbed her eyes with her thumb and forefinger.

"Look how you're sitting," Rebecca observed. "All slumped over like that, taking me to a table at the back of the shop, not looking at me. You're guilty."

"How is this conversation already going wrong when I haven't told you anything?"

"Your posture tells me everything."

"Then what is it that I have to tell you?"

"You're having an affair."

"How would I have an affair? I'm not married."

"You're having an affair with a married man, and it's been going on for some time. That's what broke up your marriage, and now that you're a free agent, he won't leave his wife. Oldest story in the book."

Rebecca sipped her latte casually, as if she had rehearsed this conversation a hundred times and had already made peace with it.

"My posture told you all of that?" Jess asked.

"Mm-hmm."

Jess planted an elbow on the table and rested her cheek against her hand, gazing at her mother. "Wow."

"I told you before, it's time to get back out there. I know you want to hold out for that one guy, but he's never leaving his wife."

"What do you think his wife is like?" Jess asked. She couldn't help herself.

"The clueless type. Lying to herself about where her husband goes. She occupies herself with the kids so she doesn't have to think about it."

"They have kids?"

"Of course, they do. All cheaters have kids. It's why they need the escape."

"Amazing," Jess said.

"I know. Well, when you've been around as long as I have." She waved a hand as if gesturing towards years of studying couples and their affairs. "I'm right, aren't I?"

"No."

"No?" Rebecca seemed doubtful. "About which part?"

"All of it."

"Come on, Jess. You can be honest with me."

"I'm gay," Jess said.

Rebecca laughed. "No, you're not."

"I am, though."

"You were married," Rebecca said. "You've been with Alan since you were a girl. I've caught you making out before. Lesbians don't make out with men like that. Aunt Lou has never once been with a man."

"I know it's confusing, Mom," Jess said. "I know it would be less confusing if I'd been a lesbian all my life, but I'm telling you that this is true now. I don't want to be with men anymore."

"Oh," Rebecca said, reaching for Jess's hand. "You're just angry at men right now. Alan wasn't the best husband. All women think being with another woman might be easier when their husbands are jerks. I didn't realize how bad he hurt you."

"No, Mom, that's not it. I'm in love with Pam. We're together."

Rebecca let go of her hand. "Your neighbor?"

"Yeah."

"Is she the one you had an affair with?"

"I didn't have an affair," Jess said. "She and I just got together a few weeks ago."

Rebecca didn't speak for a moment. Then she said, "What about the kids?"

"They know."

"You're their mother."

"I know that."

"You're going to confuse them."

"I'm not trying to confuse anybody."

"You didn't think that divorcing their father and sleeping with their neighbor would confuse them?"

"It's not like that. How I feel about Pam is different from how I've felt about anybody."

Rebecca shook her head and closed her eyes. "I can't hear this. I know that this is trendy for young people right now. My friends' grandchildren are all saying that they're bisexual and all that business. You're a grown woman with children. You need to be the model of stability and marriage."

"Oh, what like you were?" Jess said. "The reason you thought I looked guilty is because you don't know any other looks from me. You've always made me feel guilty about everything, but it's not going to work right now. I didn't cheat on Alan. I'm not with Pam just because I'm angry with men, and I want to teach my children to love who they love whoever it is. All I know about you is that you've stayed with a man you don't like for forty-five years, and it hasn't taught me anything about marriage."

Rebecca gathered her purse and stood up. "Then you haven't been paying attention."

She grasped her purse strap with one hand and pumped her other arm as if she was going to break into a run. She thrust the door open, the bell on the door ringing violently, and she stormed out of the shop.

Jess stood up and took the mugs from the table. She brought them behind the counter, where Louanne opened her arms.

"I guess I should have just had an affair," Jess said.

"Naw," Louanne said, patting her back. "He never would have left his wife."

Jess spent the rest of the day in a stunned haze. She was tired and in pain, but if she let herself feel those things, she wouldn't have been able to work, so she buried all of her anxiety and heartache in a shallow grave. It was close enough to the surface to remember and just deep enough to numb out.

Numbing was familiar. It had always gotten her through.

When Jess got home, Pam was in the kitchen mixing dough for pizza crust. The radio was set to NPR, and a reporter was interviewing an old blues musician who nobody heard of until he was seventy-three.

"Hey," Pam said, her hands working the dough in the bowl. "What's the matter? Long day?"

"Mm-hmm. Where are the kids?"

"Backyard."

"How are they?"

"They've been fine. Kevin and Alex have spent most of the day in the tree."

Jess laid her head against Pam's back and wrapped her arms around her. "Can we go hide?"

"After pizza, sure. You want to talk?"

"No. I just want to stand here like this."

Jess buried her nose into Pam's T-shirt. She allowed herself to be jostled as Pam kneaded the dough.

"I remember the dark days when I used to order pizza," Pam said. "Before a beautiful woman came into my life and chided me for not knowing how to make my own."

"She sounds judgy," Jess said, muffled against Pam's back.

"No, she's just a purist. Talk against my back again."

Jess mashed her lips against Pam until her mouth could barely move. "Liffe thisff?"

"Hee hee, that tickles."

The back door opened and Kevin walked in. Jess dropped her arms and stepped back from Pam.

"Mom," he said. "Do we have the next *Wrinkle in Time* book?"

"I don't know. I read them all when I was your age, but I might have gotten them from the library. Check the bookshelf."

"Can we go to the bookstore? I want to have it."

"I don't know, honey, I'm beat."

"Is Miss Pam sleeping over tonight?"

Pam dumped the ball of dough onto the floured counter. She and Jess glanced at each other.

"Why do you ask?" Jess said.

"Alex is sleeping over. Now that you guys are going out, is Miss Pam staying over too?"

The nights before Jess went to work, Alex would sleep over, and then Pam would come by at 4:30 in the morning so that Jess could be at the bakery for 5:00 without having to wake any of the children.

"Uh," Jess said.

"Because that would be weird," he said.

"Well, she might eventually," Jess said.

"Do you guys have sex?" Kevin asked.

"Tell you what," said Jess, louder than she'd intended. "Let's go to the bookstore after dinner."

They ate pizza and went to Barnes & Noble. Jess spent more money than she had on all of the kids; the rest of the book series for Kevin, manga for Alex, and Disney princess books for Betsy.

When they got home, Kevin laid down on his bed, holding the paperback copy of *A Wind in the Door* over his face. Jess stood in the doorway admiring her son—how relaxed his face was as he read, how he propped the pages open with his long fingers.

"Can I help you?" he asked. He kept his eyes fixed on the book, but he had a slight smile.

"Just admiring my handsome boy," Jess said.

"Gross, Mom."

"Good night," Jess sang to him. "I love you."

"Uck," he said.

As Jess turned away, Kevin said, "I love you too."

𝕤𝕤𝕤

Pam snuck in moments before Jess's alarm went off. Jess woke up to the feel of Pam pressing herself against her back, and resting her hand on Jess's stomach to pull her closer. The only light streamed in from the crack in the door. It was always dark when she got ready for work because she set her alarm for 3:00. By 5:00 people would be showing up at the bakery for fresh bread. She used to like to get up in the dark of the morning before everyone else and sit in the silence with a cup of coffee. But now Pam was beside her. Instead of popping out of bed and changing clothes like she'd done for years, she hit snooze at the blare of the alarm, closed the door all the way, and snuggled back into the crescent of Pam's embrace.

Through her shirt, Jess felt the rise and fall of Pam's belly with each breath. The rhythm lulled her back to sleep.

Pam rubbed the back of Jess's shoulder. "You're going to be late for work."

"Aunt Lou won't fire me," Jess mumbled.

"You sure about that?"

"No."

Jess rolled over and gave her a small kiss.

"You'd get fired for me?" Pam asked.

"Mm-hmm."

Jess lay a hand on Pam's hip, and slipped inside her shorts, running a thumb along the bare skin.

Pam's eyes opened wide. "You are serious about getting fired."

Jess pulled Pam's leg across her and kissed her deeply. She rolled over so that she was looking down into Pam's face. Jess brushed her fingers against Pam's cheek as if she were touching fine, thin glass.

"I love you," she said to Pam.

Pam muttered something that resembled an "I love you too" with her lips pressed against Jess's.

Jess was late.

7

Rebecca didn't come by the shop or speak to Jess for four months. Her dad called once every couple of weeks to ask her if she needed money, which he had never asked her before. Did he think that being a lesbian was expensive? He didn't call her on the day that Jess and Alan's divorce was finalized.

It was a strange feeling to mourn the death of a marriage that she initiated the execution of. Regardless, it made her sad. That was when she felt like she needed a parent, but she knew that if she called either of her parents, her dad would avoid the subject, and her mom would tell her it was her own fault anyway.

September came, and everyone got back to a busy schedule. Pam went back to the classroom. Kevin and Alex started sixth grade, and Betsy started second. October brought Jess's birthday, which her parents ignored. She surmised that it was intentional on Rebecca's part and accidental on John's since he relied on his wife to keep track of important dates for him. At first, Rebecca's silence hurt, then it was a relief, and then, as Jess's birthday came and went, it hurt again. The end of October was around the time that Rebecca would place an order with Louanne for Thanksgiving pies. But nothing.

"Maybe she doesn't want dessert this year?" Jess asked, sliding a tray of pumpkin scones into the display case.

Halloween was Louanne's favorite time of year. Aside from an array of pumpkin-flavored baked goods, she made vampire bites, which were chocolate truffles filled with raspberry filling, ghost-shaped cookies, green witch finger chocolate jelly rolls, and cupcakes decorated like eyeballs. Paper bats hung from the ceiling, plastic skeletons were arranged at a table like they were enjoying coffee, and a string of orange lights brightened the checkout counter.

Louanne wore an apron with a howling werewolf on it. "This is what your mom does, honey. It's a painful punishment when you want to see your family."

"God," Jess said. "This is what it felt like for you. All those birthdays and holidays that Mom kept you from. Why is this her punishment?"

"I don't know, but it's stupid," Louanne said. "That's why I went to Vivienne's family's parties."

"It would be hard for us to do that," Jess said. "Pam's parents live in Oregon. They said we could come by for Christmas, but the kids are spending Christmas Eve with Alan and Christmas Day with me."

"Viv and I will be there."

"Yes," Jess said. "Come boycott John and Rebecca's house with us."

"You cook better than her anyway." A timer buzzed on the counter. "That's the cookies. You said you needed two hundred?"

They were filling an order for the school. The fall festival was that weekend, and all three kids were in recitals. Usually, Jess's parents went to every grandchild event, no matter how small.

What Jess did next was something that she didn't understand and wouldn't be able to explain later. With a shaking hand, she reached for the phone on the wall, the one near the entrance to the kitchen. She shuddered at the first ring like it was a shrill alarm. She took a breath at the second. As the ring continued unanswered, sadness sunk in. She decided to leave a message.

"Hey, Mom. The fall festival is this weekend. The kids are in a recital, and I know they'd like it if you and Dad were there."

Vivienne's head poked out of the kitchen. "Is that Rebecca?"

"Jessica," Louanne said, punching numbers into the register. A bearded customer with a white box of goodies stood before her, watching the conversation. "Hang up on that asshole."

Jess spun away from Vivienne's agitated face. "It's in the gym at six o'clock on Saturday. Aunt Lou is making sugar cookies."

"She's not going to eat full-fat sugar cookies," Vivienne said. Then louder, over Jess's shoulder, at the phone, "She only drinks blood."

Jess waved her away. "It would be nice to see you."

"Like hell," Louanne said. The bearded customer lingered, holding his purchase. "You want some popcorn to go with this show?" Louanne asked him. He walked away.

"I love you," Jess added.

She hung up. Her aunts stood beside one another, glowering at her.

"What in God's name possessed you to call her?" Louanne asked.

"She's my mom," Jess said. "You never gave up on Grandma."

"But this is Rebecca," Vivienne said.

"*Rebecca* is still my mom. She's not going to come to the festival anyway."

"We understand that she's still your mom," Vivienne told her. "But if she does show up on Saturday, we're going to have to kill her."

"We won't have a choice," Louanne said.

"Oh, come on, you're not really going to kill her," Jess said. "Are you?"

"Our justice will be swift," Louanne replied.

"Slow," Vivienne said, eyes wide at the thought. "Our justice will be slow and painful."

"Guys," Jess said.

"Rebecca snubbed me and Vivienne for decades," Louanne said. "I understand that you still want her around. God help us—it's hard to stop us from wanting our mommas, no matter what kind of spoiled, ass-faced harpy they are. But hurting you is the last straw."

"I'm gonna punch her in the face," Vivienne said.

"Get her, baby," Louanne said.

"Oh my," Jess said.

⁶ᵕ ⁶ᵕ ⁶ᵕ

The school gym was a good-sized space with a basketball court, fold-out bleachers to the left and right of the court, and a stage at the far end. The coaches and PE teachers had pushed the bleachers back into the wall for the event. Kevin had been fascinated at how the bleachers could do that when he first started elementary school. These big, metal bleachers could fold and become part of the wall, undoing themselves from something enormous into something flat and unnoticeable. Folding chairs with cushy gray seats faced the stage in neat rows.

Kevin stood backstage in his butternut squash costume, watching Betsy perform as a leaf blowing in the wind. Kevin, Alex, and the rest of their sixth-grade homeroom were all dressed as various gourds who were to explain to their families and friends in the audience how they were good for humans to eat. Alex was a potato.

A boy wearing a pumpkin costume laughed at Kevin. "You look like a dick."

Kevin grimaced through the face of his pale, phallic-looking costume. The kid was right, of course. Whoever had designed the thing thought that adding a veiny texture to the squash would make it look more authentic.

"Shut up," Alex told him.

Kevin looked down at his costume and back up at the pumpkin, feigning confusion. "Am I *not* supposed to look like a penis?"

The kid made a face at the proper anatomical term. "We're supposed to be food, stupid. But you look like a dick, and she looks like a piece of shit."

Kevin forced a smile. "Thank you."

Alex said to Kevin, "I know, what a nice guy."

"You guys are weird," the pumpkin said, and went to make fun of an apple.

"Come on, everyone," their teacher called.

She was a woman about their mothers' age, skinny as a rail with a mouth full of teeth. Her teeth, to Kevin, seemed wider than the rest of her bones. Even her black, limp hair was skinny. But she was kind. She was the sort of teacher that Kevin wished he could have every year. Last year, the homeroom teacher was a tired man who disliked children and spent most of the class playing games on his phone.

Mrs. Chapman held a clipboard and scribbled things that no one else could decipher.

"Remember your lines," she told the kids.

Betsy spun in circles on stage. Kevin envied her—a leaf blowing about, giggling with the other girl and boy leaves. Some of them danced. Betsy tried her best at pirouettes. She was lucky not to have to remember lines.

Lines. He had them. What were they? He'd said them during rehearsal, and now, when he tried to recall them, it was as if he'd never known them.

He toddled around and directed his butternut body at his teacher. She was fixing a stuck zipper on the back of a carrot, her clipboard pinned in her armpit.

"Mrs. Chapman," Kevin said. "I don't remember my lines."

She lifted her arm and handed him the clipboard. "All the lines are there."

He regarded the scribbled notes. "Um," he said.

"Hurry up, Kevin," she said. "We're up next."

Kevin showed Alex the script.

"Can you read this?" he asked.

Alex peered at it. "She wrote all over it."

"She wrote over my lines," he said. "And yours."

"I have lines?" Alex asked.

"Yeah. We all do."

"Well, what are they?"

"You don't remember either?"

"I don't pay attention in rehearsal. How much can a potato have to say?" she said, an edge of panic in her voice. She swiped the clipboard. "Gimme that thing."

Jess sat rigidly between her former spouse and current girlfriend a few rows from the stage. She had been pleased at the beginning of the pageant when Alan and Cindy came to the same row with her, her aunts, and Pam. Jess was pleased, not because she wanted Alan near, but because Betsy said it would make her happy if her parents sat by each other at the festival. Alan still hadn't spent any one-on-one time with Kevin, but he seemed to have relaxed during his weekends. At least, Jess hadn't gotten any frantic phone calls that suggested otherwise.

Alan grunted a greeting, and Cindy smiled as she trailed behind him. Then he'd sat next to Jess. Jess had been holding Pam's hand. Was she supposed to keep doing that? Alan wasn't holding Cindy's hand. What were the rules of behavior between ex's who went to events with their new people? Jess should have googled some advice before she left the house.

But then, was she really going to drop Pam's hand? No. She had already come to that conclusion when they walked into the gym together. Still, she felt like all of the other parents were judging them and coming to the same conclusion as Rebecca: "But you have children." It filled her with a shame that the logical part of her thought was ridiculous. She didn't agree with her mom, and she knew that, most likely, nobody else cared.

Alan broke the silence. "Is that Rebecca and John?"

To Jess's amazement, he was right. Her parents sat on the other side of the gym. Her dad sported a dark blue suit, and her mom wore a long dress, as if they were seated at a fancy table instead of fold-out chairs in a gym. They looked regal.

"That's them," Jess said.

"Where?" Pam asked, craning her neck.

Louanne grunted and tightened her fists. Vivienne laid a hand on her arm.

"Why are they over there?" Alan asked. "Is there no room here in the lesbian section?"

"Yeah, that's it," said Jess.

Alan glanced at Jess. "Are things okay?"

Jess considered the question for a moment. He'd sounded sincere. It was a tone she hadn't heard from him in a long time.

"They're mad at me," she said. "Well, Mom's mad at me."

"The ole Rebecca freeze out?"

"Yeah."

"I always hated it when she did that," Alan said.

"She's never ignored me this long before."

"I don't know what they're doing here if they're going to ignore everybody," Vivienne said.

Two people in front of them turned around to shush them all.

"Let's just watch Betsy," Pam said. "Alex and Kevin are up next."

The piano player hit a final note, and the leaves and trees stopped spinning. The foliage lined up to take a bow.

Mrs. Chapman walked up to the microphone as the kids ran stage right, and the curtains closed. She announced the sixth-grade cornucopia of autumn fruits and vegetables. There was a minute before the curtains slid open to reveal an overflowing cornucopia painted on a backdrop. Kids dressed as seasonal produce stepped from either side of it in single file, singing a song about food. Kevin and Alex barely moved their mouths, which didn't surprise Jess. They had been complaining about this skit for weeks.

"Why are they singing?" Alan asked. "They're not first graders."

"They don't look happy about it," Cindy said.

"Why is Kevin a penis?" Louanne asked.

"Lou," Jess chided.

Pam and Vivienne laughed into their hands.

Alan's eyes widened with realization. "Oh my God, he is."

"He's butternut squash," Jess told them.

The kids stopped singing, and they each took turns explaining why they were important and what dishes they were particularly good in. Alex the potato stepped forward and said, "I'm best when I'm mashed." She slammed a fist into her open palm at the word "mashed." Then she added, "But not too lumpy." Mrs. Chapman's head appeared around the curtain. Alex perked up, listening to whatever her teacher was saying, and then she said, "I'm loaded with potassium and Vitamin B and... sour cream."

Pam covered her face and shook her head.

Alex stepped back. The piano rolled along, music anticipating a voice accompaniment. The kids on stage looked at Kevin. Mrs. Chapman reappeared around the curtain and whispered something, but Kevin ignored her.

Instead, he took Alex's hand and started to dance. Or something that resembled dancing. He spun and twirled. He pranced as best he could, clunking around in his butternut squash, Alex hopping with him. The crowd laughed, but not at him, to Jess's relief. Then other kids onstage started dancing and the piano kept up with them. Mrs. Chapman rushed over to the pianist and rolled her hand in a "wrap it up" kind of signal. The pianist played a few more notes. When the song ended, the dancing food stopped and returned to their places as if they had been playing musical chairs. Then Kevin turned to the crowd, hand in hand with Alex. He sought the hand of the boy next to him (a nice kid dressed as broccoli who wouldn't punch Kevin for touching him), and attempted a bow. The costume didn't allow him to bend. It was too top-heavy. So, he gave a gracious nod to the crowd. The kids all lined up and they bowed too, as if it had been planned.

Jess and Pam stood and applauded their children.

When the performance was over, the lights came on, sudden and harsh. The crowd blinked back at the light. Some stood and stretched as if waking up. Jess cast a glance at her parents. Her dad heaved himself out of his seat and yawned. He had probably been asleep.

Refreshment tables were set up at the front of the gym. Despite the health benefits of all the food they'd just learned about, the PTA served punch, brownies, and Flynn's Bakery cookies. Most of the adults waited for their stars to come offstage before getting a snack.

Only Betsy had stayed in costume. Kevin and Alex had left their costumes with Mrs. Chapman and hung out in their black pants and T-shirts. The adults all hugged them and told them they were brilliant.

"Nice improvisation," Pam told Alex.

"I didn't know my lines," she said.

"I could tell."

"I think the ones I came up with were much better."

"Were you supposed to dance?" Jess asked Kevin.

Kevin smiled. "No. I couldn't remember my lines either."

"Soooo, you danced?" Alan asked him.

"You made it more fun," Alex told Kevin.

"That *was* fun," Kevin said. "I think I want to try out for a play."

"In a real play, they're gonna expect you to know your lines," Louanne reminded him.

"I know. I didn't care about these lines. I was really nervous and the play was stupid. It wasn't even a play. But I liked how I felt when I was dancing and the audience liked it." He looked at Jess. "They seemed to. Did they?"

"Yeah, they did," she told him.

"It was funny," Louanne said. "Potato ballet."

Kevin, Jess noticed, hadn't stopped smiling.

"There was something about it," he said. "I don't know. I think I want to do it again."

"You want to go into theater?" Alan asked him.

"Yeah."

Alan sighed. "Okay."

Rebecca and John stepped into their circle. Rebecca swooped down to hug Betsy, without acknowledging anyone else. "You were beautiful up there. The prettiest leaf of them all."

"You watched?" Betsy asked. "Grandpa, you watched too?"

John nodded. He waved hi to everyone. Usually, it was at this point that Jess would give her dad a peck on the cheek. She didn't know what to do this time, though. She froze, and he stood there with his hands in his pockets, quiet and awkward, waiting for someone to come to him.

"And you, Kevin," Rebecca cooed. "You were the star."

"The prettiest squash of them all," Alex said.

"Don't tease him," Rebecca said. "Alan..."

Rebecca gave Alan a light hug. They made small talk, and he introduced her to Cindy. The kids asked if they could go get cookies. Alan and Cindy immediately volunteered to go with them.

Louanne poked Rebecca on the shoulder. "Hey. Stop being weird and talk to your daughter who was nice enough to invite you."

"I'm not being weird," Rebecca said.

Louanne pivoted to her brother-in-law. "John. Come here, you."

John stood still while Louanne bear-hugged him.

"Thanks for coming, Mom," Jess said.

Rebecca pulled her purse strap tightly up her shoulder and gave Jess a withering look. "Do you know how much it hurts me to be here? Seeing you and Alan sitting next to each other while you flaunt the person you had an affair with right in front of him?"

"I told you—I didn't have an affair," Jess said.

"Look what this relationship is doing to Kevin. He's confused. Mincing around onstage like a sissy."

"Don't call him that."

Rebecca waved her hand at Jess and Pam. "What is this anyway? Do you go to things together now?"

"We've always gone to things together," Jess said. "I don't understand why you're so upset. You don't have a problem with Aunt Lou and Vivienne anymore."

"Louanne didn't push Vivienne on us, and she didn't have kids to think about."

"*Push* me on you?" Vivienne asked.

"Rebecca," John said.

"This isn't hurting the kids," Jess said. "I wouldn't get into a relationship that would hurt them."

"You have no idea what you're doing to them," Rebecca said.

"Rebecca," John said, more loudly. "It's time to go."

Rebecca raised a knuckle to the corner of her eye and sniffed. "All right."

John crossed over to Jess and kissed her on the cheek. He nodded to Pam, and followed his wife towards the door.

Jess shook, her mother's words causing an avalanche inside of her. How could her mom not know Jess well enough to believe that she would make decisions that would hurt the kids? And why wasn't it important to her that Jess was happy with Pam? Mixed in with those thoughts was an undercurrent of the question, "What if she's right?"

"I'm sorry she did that," Jess said to Pam.

"You've got nothing to be sorry about," Pam said.

"Rebecca does," Louanne said.

She charged after her sister.

Louanne caught up with them in the parking lot and hollered at Rebecca to stop. The couple stood near their car. Tears streamed down Rebecca's cheeks.

"Not now, Louanne," she said.

"Yes, now. I should have brought Vivienne to everything. Every Christmas, birthday, first Communion, and all that crap. But I introduced Vivienne to you, Momma, and Daddy—and you all were awful to her. So, I protected her from you. From that. From what just happened in there. I wasn't doing it to keep you from feeling uncomfortable.

"We wanted kids, Vivienne and me. It's people like you who kept us from it, who made us scared. I wish every day now that we'd gone ahead and done it anyway. Don't you dare try to make Jess feel ashamed ever again. Don't you dare ever do to her what you did to me."

Louanne stormed back into the gym without letting Rebecca get a word in. She thought of what her mother had told her just before she died, the thing she'd never told anyone, not even Vivienne, and she held it close to her.

Her family was near the refreshment table. Alan was surrounded by the kids who were talking at him all at once. Jess, Pam, Cindy, and Vivienne were chatting and sipping punch.

She watched them all for a moment before Vivienne noticed her and waved her over.

"What did Rebecca say?" Vivienne asked.

"Nothing," Louanne said. "I just told her off."

"I wish I had done that," Jess said, still trembling.

"I can't believe she said all that to you," Cindy told her. "I don't know how I could go on if my mother cut me off."

"It happened to me too," Louanne said, sliding an arm around Vivienne's waist. "You know what? Fuck her. If Rebecca doesn't want to be part of this family, that's her fault."

8

Kevin began writing a play. He sat on the floor with a notebook and pen, back against his bed, and wrote. He set it in New York because things seemed to happen there. After writing for a while, he jumped up to go find Alex and Betsy. They were in the front yard raking leaves.

"Hey guys," Kevin said. "I'm writing a play. Want to be in it?"

"Yes," Betsy said eagerly. "Give me a dancing part."

"Make me a superhero," Alex said. "Like Captain Marvel."

"My play doesn't have dancing or people with superpowers."

"What's it about then?" Alex asked.

"Just people."

"That's boring," Betsy said. "You should put more things in it."

"There's a murder," Kevin told them.

"Murder's good," Betsy said.

"Can I be the victim?" Alex asked.

"Show me how you die."

"Okay," Alex said. "Betsy, pretend to kill me."

Betsy swung the rake around and slapped Alex on the back of the head. Alex stuck out her tongue with a "bleh!" and crumpled into the leaves.

"Not bad," Kevin said. "But I was thinking something more like this."

He made a finger gun and pointed it at his chest. He staggered back, dropping the notebook and pen.

"You'll regret this, Reginald," he wheezed. "I am your fiancé's father!"

He fell face down into the leaves. Alex and Betsy applauded.

"What happens when his fiancé finds out?" Alex asked.

"She stays with him and doesn't ever tell anybody. Their secret drives her insane."

"Nice."

"Let's practice going insane," said Betsy.

She ran in a circle, arms flailing over her head and screaming.

The scream stopped Jess from picking up socks from Betsy's floor, and she looked out the window.

"Pam," she called. "Should we be concerned about the children?"

Pam came into the room and peeked out the blinds. All three kids were running in circles, hollering, and falling down.

"Hmm," said Pam. "Didn't we tell them to bag those leaves?"

Jess sighed. "Yes."

"At least Kevin came out of his room," Pam said.

"Now they're having a leaf fight."

"That was inevitable," Pam said. "Kids can't be around a pile of something without throwing part of the pile at each other. Case in point..."

She pulled a sock from Jess's arms and tossed it in her face. Jess retaliated. The sock battle was brief, but merciless.

It ended with socks all over Betsy's floor and a long kiss. Pam rested her cheek against Jess's and took a breath that ended with an "mmm." The hum of it against Jess's skin made her tremble.

The honk of the F150 in the driveway killed the moment.

"Did you know that Alan was coming over?" Pam asked.

"No."

The kids seemed surprised, too. Betsy didn't run into his arms like usual – not right away. She paused, a mess of crinkly leaves in her hair. Jess wondered if Betsy, like Jess, had come to worry about Alan's unexpected visits. They usually meant that he was irate about something.

Jess and Pam hurried outside.

Alan hopped down from the cab and lifted Betsy into a hug. He set her down and planted his hands on his hips. "Looks like you guys have a good leaf battle going on there."

"They're supposed to be raking it into a bag," Jess said. "What brings you here?"

Alan shrugged. "I was in the neighborhood and thought I'd drop by. I was wondering if Kevin might want to come to lunch with me."

"Just you and me?" Kevin asked.

"Yeah. How about it?"

Kevin considered how much energy it would take to pretend to be someone who enjoyed spending time with his dad. "I already ate lunch."

"Ice cream, then," his dad said.

"I want to come," Betsy said.

"Next time, it can be just you and me. Today is your brother's turn." He looked to Jess as if suddenly remembering that she was there. "Is that okay?"

"Yeah, it's okay with me," she said.

"Great. Hop in, Kev."

"The name 'Kev' is for the Neanderthals at school," Kevin said.

"Come on, *Kevin*," Alan told him.

"Let me go get my book," Kevin said, dashing towards the house.

"You don't need," Alan started to say, but the boy was already at the door.

"He takes a book everywhere," Jess said. "It's like his security blanket."

"Will you bring me back ice cream?" Betsy asked.

"When I take you, you'll have some," Alan assured her.

Kevin walked out with a paperback in his hand. Alan told Jess he'd have Kevin back in a couple of hours and climbed into the truck.

Jess watched them drive away. Which one of them would carry the conversation? She got the impression that neither of them was speaking. They weren't looking at each other. Maybe Alan was waiting for Kevin to say something. Alan wasn't a patient man. When he finally got antsy and opened his mouth, would he ask Kevin if he liked girls? It was Jess who had suggested that Alan spend time with Kevin to get to know him, but she wished she'd told him what she thought was okay to say and what wasn't. Did Alan know how much his questions, his tone of voice, and body language could hurt Kevin? How a look of disgust, even for a moment, could shape a child's life, like how a small amount of pressure on the body at a certain angle could break a bone in one seemingly nonthreatening, nonviolent movement.

Jess had the impulse to call Alan and insist that he turn around and pick her up. She could sit between them in the truck to be the translator. "What your dad means is..." "Kevin said that because..."

She set her hands on her hips and blew out a big puff of air, hoping they would find the right words to understand each other.

᯿ ᯿ ᯿

There was an ice cream stand in the park, not far from Jess's house. Alan left the truck under the shade of an oak tree and walked with Kevin along the pond to the ice cream cart. Kevin plodded along with his head bent to his book.

"You gonna read the whole time?" Alan asked.

"I like reading and walking," Kevin told him.

"Huh."

Kevin lowered the book. "It's not weird."

"I didn't say it was weird."

"You said 'huh' like it was weird."

"Jesus, kid," Alan said.

They arrived at the cart. A teenager not much older than Kevin asked them what they wanted. Alan picked chocolate, and Kevin got strawberry. Alan led them to a bench at the foot of the duck pond. Kevin bit a chunk of strawberry out of the scoop.

"How's school going?" Alan asked.

"Fine."

"Grades are okay?"

"Yeah."

"You always did have good grades."

"There's a portal where you can check them if you really want to know," Kevin said.

"Naw, I trust ya."

They ate their ice cream.

"How are you doing with your mom and Miss Pam being together?"

"All right."

"It's not strange?"

"A little."

Alan shook his head. "I wouldn't have guessed. I mean, your mom, when we first started going out, she..." he cleared his throat. "Anyway, I was surprised. Does school know?"

"My teacher does. There's another kid in my class with two moms."

"It's a thing nowadays, I suppose. They living together yet?"

"Is that what you wanted to talk to me about?" Kevin asked.

Alan lowered his ice cream and looked out at the ducks. Chocolate dripped down the cone.

"I want to know you better," Alan said.

"But you're asking me about Mom."

"It affects you, doesn't it? Who she gets together with?"

"I guess. She didn't ask me questions when you hooked up with Cindy."

"Watch it," Alan warned.

"Sorry."

Alan made a face, as if he was trying to force the irritation out of it. "I haven't been around a lot lately,"

"It's okay," Kevin said.

"Well, don't you want to hang out with me?"

"*You* think I'm weird."

Alan shook his head. "You're still my son. Maybe you just need to spend some time with your old dad."

"Do you think that will make me less weird?"

"Might be better than spending all your time with lesbians."

"Don't talk about Mom and Miss Pam like that," Kevin said. Then he remembered his father's slap and added, "Please."

"It's a fact," Alan said. "They are two lesbians, aren't they?"

"What does that have to do with me liking to read?"

"Well," Alan said. "What other things do you like?"

"Acting and writing."

"What else?"

"Climbing the tree in the backyard."

"Climbing's great," Alan said. "I could take you rock climbing."

"That might be fun," Kevin said.

"Really?" Alan brightened. "That would be something you want to do?"

"Yeah, I'll give it a try."

"I'll take you next weekend, then."

Kevin shoved the last of his ice cream cone into his mouth. Alan passed him a napkin for his fingers.

"How long are we going to stay out here?" Kevin asked.

"I told your mom about a couple of hours." He checked his watch. "It's been twenty minutes."

"Can I read?"

"I can just take you back if you want."

"No. I think this would be a nice place to read."

"Oh," Alan said. "You really want to do that?"

"Yeah."

"All right. For a bit."

Alan pulled his phone from his pocket and scrolled through the news. Kevin watched him out of the corner of his eye, looking for any irritated body language that would signal a soon departure. Seeing none, he allowed himself to settle into his book.

Three sentences in, his dad said, "Is this what you really do all the time?"

The question wasn't an accusation. His dad sounded genuinely curious. Still, Kevin kept his eyes on the page.

"Yes," Kevin said.

"And you don't get bored?"

"No. I read when you lived with us."

"Not this much."

"I did."

"Okay," Alan said, "So, your mom's gay and you're a bookworm. Is Betsy really into *Frozen* or did I get that wrong?"

"Unfortunately, you're right about that."

"Ha! So, what's good about that book?"

Kevin told him the plot of *A Swiftly Tilting Planet,* the third book in the *Wrinkle in Time* series. He talked about how much he identified with Meg, especially in the first book. At first, he wasn't going to tell his dad that part, but he seemed to really be listening, and that made Kevin want to tell him.

"Sounds interesting," Alan said.

"I could read it out loud," Kevin said.

Alan took a breath. He shoved his phone in his pocket and crossed his arms. "Go for it."

"Really?"

"Yeah, it'll be like a book on tape or something."

Kevin began to read, "'It was still twilight when they reached the flat rock. They sat, and the stone still held the warmth of the day's sun...'"

He brought Kevin home about an hour and a half later. Jess was sitting in the armchair and Pam sat long ways on the couch, both reading by the lamplight on the end table.

Jess lowered her book. "Did you guys have a nice time?"

"Sure did," Alan said. He tousled Kevin's hair. "Lemme talk to your mom a second."

Kevin was grateful to run into the backyard to find Alex. Pam excused herself.

Alan put his hands on his hips and brought his left foot forward. Jess smiled. He'd been striking that pose for twenty years, and she had always thought it made him look gay.

"Y'all read together?" Alan asked. "I see where Kevin gets it."

"Did you *really* have a nice time with him?" Jess asked.

"It was a little awkward, but not bad. I want to spend some more one-on-one time with him if that's okay."

"Of course," Jess said, a little bit surprised.

"I know we don't have much in common, he and I. But you said I should spend time with him, and Cindy told me I should spend time with him, so I figured I probably should. I just...I don't want things to turn out with us like what happened with you and your mom."

Jess nodded. "That's good, Alan."

"Is she still not talking to you?"

"No."

"Well. Maybe she'll come around with you like she did with Louanne."

"Maybe."

"I have to go. I'm taking Cindy to some wine bar that just opened up."

"You don't drink wine."

"Yeah, well. The things you do, you know? See y'all."

Jess often wondered why parental acceptance was so important. What did it matter if a mother or a father didn't accept someone? Maybe when you're a baby, she thought, but what difference did it make when you're a grown person who doesn't need a parent to survive?

She didn't know, but her mother's continued silence was painful. Rebecca didn't call Jess after the play. She didn't answer when Jess called her on Christmas. There was no happy new year. Jess's grief over her mother's silence confused her. She didn't actually like Rebecca's company. She should have felt free. Her dad still called, and sometimes stopped by the bakery, but he would ask Jess not to tell Rebecca he'd been there. As if visiting Jess was forbidden.

On New Year's Day, she tended the garden with Pam instead of dragging the kids to her mom's house for blackeye peas and pork roast. The birds of paradise had survived a hard freeze that had killed off half of their other plants. Jess had been worried about how they'd do, and was pleased to find the two strange flowers going strong, heads lifted proudly towards the winter sun.

"We covered the other plants too," Jess said, beholding the wilted, brown vegetation between the birds of paradise. "I wonder why they died, but the Birds didn't."

"I don't know. I still have a lot to learn about gardening," Pam said. She slipped on rough gloves and crouched down to pull the dead things from the dirt. "I know that we can plant annuals right now, but that's where my winter planting expertise ends."

Jess was impressed with how easily Pam rolled with things. More precisely, how Pam rolled with her mistakes. Jess felt guilty about the plants they'd lost, the ones that relied on her to take care of them. She felt like she couldn't be trusted to take care of such fragile things if she didn't know how to do it perfectly. But Pam, after losing almost a whole garden, pulled on her gloves and got rid of withered plants, full of talk about what they could grow next.

"What do you think about lavender?" Pam asked. She studied the freshly dug dirt as if she was visualizing the lavender and considering how it would look.

"We can do that?" Jess asked. "We can grow lavender?"

"Yeah, why not?"

"When I think of lavender, I think of a bar of soap."

"It's a plant before it's soap."

"I've just never thought about where it came from."

Pam took her phone from her back pocket. "It's pretty. Lemme show you. It'll look great in the garden." Pam walked sideways on her knees and pressed her side against Jess. She held out her phone, which featured a large, thriving lavender plant in the sunshine. Pam rested her cheek against Jess's so that Jess could feel the word "See," when Pam said it.

Jess laughed. "I know what lavender flowers look like. There's always a picture of it on the soap."

Pam turned her head so that her lips were against Jess's cheek. "I just wanted an excuse to be closer to you."

Jess took a quick glance around the yard, and with no kids in sight, she met Pam's kiss.

It was quick. Jess couldn't fully relax into a kiss when there was a possibility of one of the kids interrupting at any moment. She couldn't let herself go. She was always on alert when they were there, even if she and Pam were outside and the kids were inside. It was hard to escape into a romantic feeling when she was in mom mode. Mom mode wasn't sexy.

They were interrupted, but not by the kids. Lindsey stood by the chain link fence, calling out to them.

"Hey, you two," she said. She had a conspiratorial smile. "What are y'all up to?"

"Trying to salvage what's left of the garden," Jess said.

"Oh yeah, that damn freeze killed my geraniums. I just came to tell y'all that your kids are at my house."

"When did they go over there?" Pam asked.

"I don't think it's been long. I heard a ruckus in the backyard and when I checked the boys were playing with your three. Looked like they were pretending to be in a movie or something."

"Kevin's been writing plays for the girls to perform," Jess said.

"Damn," Lindsey said, laughing. "Tom was already saying that he hoped this doesn't mean our boys are too into theater. You know what I mean?"

"No," said Jess, even though she did.

"Oh, you know men and their sons," she said, waving her hand. "I don't care whether our boys are gay or straight or whatever. But Tom worries."

"Is Tom uncomfortable around gay people?" Jess asked.

Lindsey suddenly seemed a little panicked. She held out a hand as if pulling Jess from a wrong idea. "No, no, no. Not at all. Well. Other men, maybe. But not women. Definitely not you two. If anything, he wishes you two were a little more cozy with one another when you come over." She belly-laughed and added, "Men."

Jess laughed nervously along with Lindsey. Pam's expression remained stern.

Lindsey smiled at them. "It's so sweet to see you two together. I'll send the kids home before dinner."

"Great," Pam said.

"Thanks," said Jess.

When Lindsey was out of earshot, Jess said, "That's just great."

"What part?" Pam asked. "That Kevin is bringing culture to Lindsey's kids or that Tom is homophobic and he and Lindsey fetishize queer women?"

"Do you think that's what people think when we hold hands or kiss in public?" Jess asked. "Are they waiting for us to turn into porn or something?"

"Some of them, unfortunately," Pam said. "But not everybody."

"I have a hard enough time relaxing without that kind of pressure."

"What kind of pressure?"

"To be something or someone I'm not."

Pam took a breath. "It doesn't ultimately matter what they think."

"I know. I don't feel that way around strangers. Just people I know who've known me. I want them to know that I'm still me."

Pam brushed a lock of hair behind Jess's ear. "I wish I could calm down the part of you that cares what people think."

"Me too. I'm like my parents in that way, I guess."

The next morning, John came into the bakery carrying a duffle bag on his shoulder. It was after the rush, so there were just four people, retiree age, each at their own table with newspapers spread open, sipping coffee. Billie Holiday played "Summertime" over the loudspeaker.

"Dad," Jess said, coming out from behind the counter. She kissed his cheek. "It's good to see you."

When he didn't return the enthusiasm, Jess retreated to her workspace. "Coffee?"

"To go," John said.

"Work trip?" Jess asked.

"I'm leaving your mother," he said. "Thought you should know."

9

"You're leaving her?" Jess asked.

John nodded.

"Does Mom know?"

"I told her first, naturally."

Louanne stepped out of the kitchen, holding up her phone. "Oh, she knows. She sent me five messages in the last ten seconds."

Vivienne toweled off her powdery hands with her apron and peeked at Louanne's phone.

"I can't believe I'm asking this," Jess said to John, "but why?"

"I want to talk to my daughter," John said. "See my grandchildren."

"But...you never really call or come over."

"I didn't have to. Your mom did all that. Now she's not." He raised his eyes to the aunts. "I never approved of how she treated you both. I let her handle it because you were her family, but I thought it was cruel."

"I appreciate that, John," Vivienne said, her voice catching, looking like she might cry, but she just gripped her apron in her fist.

"Yes, siree," Louanne hooted. "My brother-in-law's found his balls!"

Rebecca threw the door open. The part of her mother's presence that startled Jess the most wasn't the force with which she burst through the door, or the wild look on her face, or the way that she stormed over to Jess first when she was supposedly looking for her husband. It was the fact that she was wearing pajamas (maroon silk top and bottoms), tennis shoes, a jacket, and no makeup. Rebecca never even stepped outside the house to check the mail unless her face was on.

"Did you put him up to this?" Rebecca snapped at Jess.

Jess recoiled. "No."

Rebecca shifted the glare to Louanne and Vivienne. "You?"

"No one put me up to anything," John said.

"But I have been hoping he'd leave you for years," Louanne said.

Rebecca grimaced at her sister. "Shut up, Lou."

"Rebecca," John said. "Don't make a scene."

The four customers in the café were trying to play it cool by sneaking peeks at the action over their newspaper or coffee.

The anger on Rebecca's face dissolved into misery. "You can't go. We're married. We're not like other people. That means something to us."

"I don't want to talk about this here," John said quietly.

"I won't give you a divorce," Rebecca said, her body shaking like a plucked, tight string.

John pinched the bridge of his nose. He set his duffel on the ground and took the stool next to him. Rebecca sat without averting her gaze, as if he'd disappear if she turned her head.

"You're a mean person, Rebecca," he said to her.

"I make you breakfast every morning."

"I don't ask you to."

"I make your doctor appointments, I clean your clothes, I remind you when it's your mother's birthday."

"I know."

"You wouldn't have gone to the dentist in the last thirty years if it wasn't for me."

"Rebecca—"

"I've been faithful to you," she said.

"You've ignored Jess. You told me to shut her out."

"How else will she learn?"

"Learn what?" Jess said.

"Your father and I are talking," Rebecca said.

"Jess is a grown woman," John said. "We can't teach her lessons like she's a child anymore."

"She's ruined her life. We can't pretend that we approve."

Without raising his voice, he said, "You don't speak for me."

"You approve of her leaving her husband and becoming gay? With two children to take care of?"

John shook his head. "You're still talking about Jess. That's not the problem. You aren't a nice person anymore."

"You're leaving me because I'm not nice?"

"Yes."

"I seem to recall that when we first got together you liked that I wasn't a meek, blushing flower. You liked that I said what I thought."

"But you weren't mean. Forty years ago, I never would have imagined that you would cut off one of the kids - for *any* reason. And you know that I never liked the way you and your mother treated Louanne. Family is family."

"I'm your wife," Rebecca said. "I'm the most important part of your family. We used to feel the same way about that. Remember? The hierarchy is God, then spouse, then children, then others, then self."

"God, spouse, children, and others don't want you to be cruel."

Louanne set a paper cup of coffee before him. "Still take cream?"

"Black," he said, slurping a sip. "Milk doesn't sit right with me anymore."

"Yes, Louanne, let's talk about his dietary restrictions," Rebecca said.

"You're just mad because I'm not giving you coffee."

"Tell your sister what you want to do for our anniversary," John said to Rebecca.

"Rent a beach house in Gulf Shores," Rebecca said. "What's bad about that?"

"You said you wanted it to be a family trip," John reminded her. He pointed at the ladies. "Do they know about it?"

Jess, Louanne, and Vivienne confirmed that they did not know about the trip.

"You only invited Toby and Amber, and they don't want to go because we're leaving out everyone else. It'll just be you and me in a big, empty house. It'll be your fault for driving everyone away and my fault for going along with it, and I won't do it anymore, I won't."

The customers weren't pretending to ignore them anymore. They were all watching, nibbling their pastries like it was popcorn.

Rebecca leaned against the counter, tired, as if she'd just run a long way. To Jess, there was something in the small movement that looked defeated.

"If I invited them, would you come back home?" Rebecca asked.

"I'd consider it," John said.

"What if they don't even want to go?" Rebecca said.

"Ask us and find out," Louanne said. "That's how these things work. You invite people, and they let you know."

Rebecca rubbed her thumb and forefinger together. She glanced nervously around the bakery. Louanne crossed her arms and Vivienne raised her eyebrows at Rebecca. Jess bookended Louanne.

"John and I," Rebecca said, "would be honored if you joined us—"

"Don't talk to me like you're a goddamn greeting card," Louanne said. "Just ask."

"Do you want to come to the beach or not?" Rebecca spat.

"When is it?"

"June 25th through the 29th."

"I'll have to check my calendar."

"Oh, for God's sake."

"We run a business, goddammit. I have to check."

Louanne tapped her phone, scrolling through her calendar.

"All right," Rebecca said. Looking down at her feet, she asked, "What about you?"

"I just told you, I have to check," Louanne told her.

"Not you. Jess."

"I don't know that you're talking to me if you don't look at me," Jess said.

Rebecca looked at Jess. "Will you come?"

"As long as I can bring Pam and all the kids. Hers and mine."

"You like Pam well enough," John said to Rebecca.

"When she was Jess's friend."

"Mom," Jess said. "She's the same person."

Rebecca sighed. "If it's important to you, she can come."

"She is important to me," Jess said.

"All right," Louanne said, smiling victoriously at her phone. "I can take off."

"Both of us?" Vivienne asked.

Jess couldn't tell if Vivienne's tone was wishful or afraid.

"Yeah, girl, I'm not going without you," Louanne said. "We can get away for a couple of days."

"Good," said John. He shouldered his duffel and took his coffee. "I leased an apartment down the road. I'll text you the address for my mail."

"You're not still going, are you?" Rebecca asked.

"I need time to think, Rebecca."

Rebecca laid a hand on his arm. "You'll think about coming back?"

John considered the hand that held him. The touch, it seemed, gave him pause. "I will." He turned a solemn gaze on Jess. "Can I join your family for dinner tonight?"

"Oh. Um. Sure."

He nodded, and without another word, he left the café. Rebecca grasped at the collar of her pajamas and glared at Jess. Jess waited for her to say something, but she didn't. Instead, she did something Jess had never seen her mother do. Rebecca sat down and cried.

🙚 🙚 🙚

Pam pulled a roasted chicken from the oven. She set it down on a cooling rack next to the salad that Jess was mixing. The kids were at the table—Betsy colored while Kevin and Alex watched their mothers.

"You've never seen your mom cry?" Pam asked Jess.

"Never," Jess said.

"I've never seen Grandma cry either," Kevin said.

"Wow," Alex said. "My grandma cries constantly."

"It's true," Pam said. "Commercials, weddings, births, football games, graduations."

"She cries when I make her stuff, too," Alex said.

Betsy filled in a colorless princess's dress with a bright yellow. "I made my grandma a Rudolf ornament one time. She looked confused."

"You used too much glue," Kevin told her.

Betsy stopped coloring. "Gluing a poof ball to a clothespin is hard."

"The googly eyes are impossible," Alex said.

"I know!"

"Mom," Kevin said. "What are we going to do when Grandpa gets here?"

Jess had wondered the same thing. "Eat?" she guessed.

"Maybe he'll talk."

"Guys," Jess said. She brought the salad to the center of the table and sat. "Before your grandpa gets here—what do you think about going to the beach with Grandma, Grandpa, Aunt Lou, and Uncle Toby this summer?"

"So," Kevin said. "Are Grandma and Grandpa staying together, then?"

"Let's assume they are," Jess replied.

"Good. I don't want them to break up."

"Me neither," Betsy said.

"You *want* to go to the beach then?"

"Can mom and I come?" Alex asked.

Pam brought the chicken to the table and sat next to Jess. Jess took her hand. "Yeah, all of us will go together."

There was a knock at the door.

"I'll get it," Betsy said, abandoning the coloring book and running to the door with a yellow crayon in her fist. A few seconds later, Betsy squealed, "Come see what I'm making for you."

Jess didn't hear her dad's response, if he gave any. Betsy talked all the way from the door to the table, pulling John's hand behind her.

He gave the table a smile. "Hello."

"Sit next to me," Betsy said. "I'll show you. She's not done yet."

"You can finish it after you eat," Jess told her.

"But—"

"Dinner first." Jess came around to her dad and gave him a kiss. "Hi, Dad."

"It's good to see everyone," he said.

And then no one spoke or moved. They all stared at John, which seemed to make him incredibly uncomfortable. Jess felt the seconds tick by. She knew she should stop staring but couldn't. She thought she should say something but she couldn't do that either.

Betsy handled it for her.

"Can Dad and Cindy come to the beach too?" Betsy asked him.

"Oh," John said.

"Maybe another time," Jess told her.

"But Grandpa doesn't mind."

John cleared his throat. "That's really up to your mom."

"I don't want to go without Dad," Betsy said.

"Don't you think it would be weird if your dad was there?" Alex said.

"No," Betsy said. "You just think that because he's not *your* dad."

"No. I think it because he has a girlfriend and," Alex motioned towards Jess and Pam, "they're together."

"So? Mom said it's a family trip and she told me that Dad would never stop being my dad. So, he should come."

"That's true," Jess told her. "But just not this trip."

"My mom and dad are divorced," Betsy told John. "Are you getting divorced?"

Jess began cutting the chicken. "Kevin, can you get the rice from the stove? Betsy, pass the salad to Grandpa."

"Do you like salad?" Betsy asked him.

John nodded. Betsy grabbed the bowl and handed it to him.

"It's all yours," she said.

"Grandpa, can we go snorkeling?" Kevin asked.

"I don't think they have that there," Jess said.

"Surfing?"

"I want to go surfing!" Alex said. "I want to do that thing where you surf through a whole wave and then it falls over on you and goes phhhhhh!"

She mimicked a wave crashing over her.

"Why would you want to do that?" Kevin asked.

"It would look cool."

"Do you surf, Grandpa?" Betsy asked.

"I—"

"I'm going to build the biggest sandcastle anyone has ever built," Kevin said.

"I'm going to smash it," said Alex.

"Like hell," Kevin said.

"Kevin!" Jess said.

"I'm eleven, I can swear."

"No, you can't. Not at the table and definitely not when we've got company."

"Do you swear, Grandpa?" Betsy asked.

John took a forkful of chicken. He ate quietly while the kids asked him question after question without waiting for an answer.

When they were done, he slid his chair back. Betsy grabbed his forearm.

"Wait," she said. "I need to finish your picture."

He acquiesced, laying his hands on his knees.

"Do we seem crazy to you?" Alex asked.

John shook his head. "I have four younger brothers."

"I didn't know you have brothers," Kevin said.

"Four *loud* brothers," Jess said.

John nodded. "I didn't have a quiet meal until I got married."

Betsy gave her picture a finishing flourish, tore the page from the book, and handed it to him. "For you."

"Thank you," he said, staring at the picture as if he were interpreting complicated art.

"Will you come back?" Betsy asked.

Jess scooted her chair back, the scraping sound drowning out John's answer. "Tell Grandpa good night and get ready for your bath."

She gave him a quick, tight hug and scampered off. John patted Kevin's shoulder.

"Want to take anything with you, Dad?" Jess asked.

"No, thank you."

She walked beside him to the door. "I didn't know if you'd have food there. I don't ever remember you cooking."

"The place has a stove," he said. "Thought I'd try my hand at it."

Jess whispered so the kids couldn't hear, "I'm sorry about all the questions."

"They're kids."

"They were excited to see you."

"You," said John, "have a lovely family."

"Really?" Jess said.

"They feel comfortable enough to speak their mind," John said. "That's good."

"I thought you were miserable."

He patted her on the cheek and opened the door. "Until next time."

As John pulled out of the driveway, Jess's phone rang. It was a number she hadn't seen in months.

"Mom?" Jess said.

"Is he there?" Rebecca asked.

"Who?"

"Your dad. He came over, didn't he? He can't cook for himself. He had to go somewhere."

"Yeah, he came over. Brought a couple of call girls with him. They brought cake."

"I'm not in the mood for your jokes," Rebecca said. "Did he say anything about me?"

"I'm not going to be the intermediary for you and Dad."

"You would if you cared about us staying together. Now that you don't care about your own marriage, you don't care about anyone else's either?"

"That," Jess said, "is the kind of stuff that Dad was talking about when he said you've become mean. You want my marriage advice? Work on that."

"Ha! *Your* advice."

Rebecca hung up the phone. Jess stood by the door, her arms hung at her sides. She'd made so many bad decisions. Maybe her input really was no good. After all, what did she know? There was a time she'd honestly believed that she and Alan would be together forever.

"Whatever," Jess said to herself, "whether I'm right or wrong, she's still a mean son of a bitch."

கை கை கை

John came to dinner every Thursday. It was still awkward. He didn't say much, but it was nice having him there, even though Jess felt forced to make conversation, and every time he left, she was convinced that he wouldn't come back.

Rebecca called for a few weeks, trying to get information out of Jess. Was he seeing anybody? Did he look miserable? Did he talk about her? Jess answered at first. In the fear that her father wouldn't come back, she took her mother's calls as if both parents might slip away. But after the first few Thursdays became consistent, Jess began ignoring her calls. What was the point? Rebecca wasn't calling to talk to Jess.

Without her mother's interrogations, Jess was able to enjoy the peace of her dad's company. Until one Thursday when she walked him to his car and he asked her a question. The sun had set. The streetlights gave the cul de sac a sleepy glow.

John crossed his arms and leaned against his car. "Would you mind if your mom joined us for dinner next week?"

Jess's answer was automatic. "What does she want?"

"I think she just wants to see everybody."

"Hmm."

"She asked if I would give her a chance."

"Do you want to?"

"We're coming up on forty years together. Seems foolish to not give it a shot. And I would be lying if I said I didn't miss her."

"What do you miss about her?"

"Oh, her...little ways."

Jess waited for him to elaborate. When he didn't, she leaned against the car next to him.

"I don't know if I want to give her another shot," Jess said. "Besides, she wouldn't be coming over to see me or the kids. She's just trying to get you back."

"Well, it's your decision. I understand if you don't want to see her."

"Do you really miss her?" Jess asked. "Honestly. You're not just saying that because she's wearing you down?"

"I miss home."

"That's not the same thing."

"Home isn't just a house. It's what we've built together. I just wanted her to stop tearing it apart by being...how she was being."

"I don't know, Dad. I see what you're saying. I just don't know if she can change."

"I don't know either. But I told her I'd give her a chance."

ᏕᏫ ᏕᏫ ᏕᏫ

Dinner was creepy. Rebecca arrived shortly after John, ringing the doorbell moments after John came in. Jess wondered if her mom had sat in her car and waited for her dad to go inside so she wouldn't have to be alone with Jess and Pam. Rebecca wore a constant smile, complimented the food, and told the kids how beautiful they were and how big they were getting, as if not having seen them in years. She asked Pam and Jess how work was going. She didn't make much eye contact, or say anything to John. She'd sat across from him, which made the avoidance of eye contact noticeable, though Jess wondered if she were the only one who noticed. She might have been the only one paying attention, hypervigilant about whatever game Rebecca was playing.

After she ate the last bite of food on her plate, she said, "I wish I didn't, but I *have* to go. I've been doing yoga before bed, and it's working wonders for my sleep. Jess, do you ever practice yoga? It's good exercise. Remember that, girls," she said to Alex and Betsy, "as you get older you'll have to start paying closer attention to your figure. Yoga is fabulous for the figure without giving you too much muscle."

"There's nothing wrong with the girls having muscle," Jess said.

Rebecca almost spoke. She opened her mouth and clapped it shut like a gasping fish. The smile came back. "True."

She stood up, and John stood with her. Not to leave, but out of some old-fashioned respect that Jess never understood.

"Well," Rebecca said. "It was good to see you all. John," she said, finally looking at him, "maybe next time I can cook you dinner."

"Maybe so," he said.

Jess didn't walk her mother to the door. As soon as she heard it shut, she said, "Jesus Christ, that was awful."

"Grandma was nice," Betsy said.

"That's why it was weird," Kevin said.

"It's like she was making herself like us," Alex said.

"Exactly."

"Girls," Jess said. "Staying skinny isn't the point of yoga."

"I know that," Alex said.

"She said it was for sleep," John said.

"Then what was all that stuff about the girls keeping up their figures?"

"Isn't that the kind of tips women give each other?" he asked.

"No, Dad! That's the toxic crap we feed each other to keep us hating our bodies."

"Is that some new thing?" he asked. "That's all I've ever heard women talk about."

"Are you serious, Dad? You've been coming over here for weeks, and all you've heard me and Pam talk about is staying thin?"

"Sometimes," he said.

"He's right," Pam said. "We do talk about it a lot."

The kids mumbled in agreement.

"Well," Jess said. "We shouldn't. I don't want you kids thinking it's the only important thing about you."

"I agree with Betsy," John said. "She was nice."

"Do you think she was being genuine?" Jess asked.

"She's doing what I asked. That's all I know."

Pam sipped her wine. "I think it's great."

"*You* think she was being genuine?" Jess asked.

"Who cares? That's the nicest she's ever been to me. If it's because she's had a spiritual awakening, good! If it's because she's getting her act together to win this guy back and it means she has to be sweet to the gays, good!"

"Well put," John said.

"But," Jess said, having lost her one supporter. "You're not going back to her, are you, Dad?"

"I'll go to dinner," he said. "We'll see."

"Any day but a Thursday, right?" Pam asked him.

"Of course," John said.

"Good."

After John left, the kids cleaned the kitchen, and Jess asked Pam to sit with her in the bedroom so that they could talk without being overheard.

Pam leaned against the headboard, legs crossed. Jess paced beside her, stepping around two piles of socks, one white and one colored, that she'd been meaning to sort through.

"Why did you defend my mom?" Jess asked.

"He's going back to her, Jess. You can tell."

"He hasn't said that he is."

"He's saying he misses home and he misses her. Now she's putting on the sweet act."

"But that's the thing. It's just an act."

"We know that, but it's not up to us whether or not he goes back to her. He most likely is. If that happens, you want him to keep coming over, right?"

Jess set her hands on her hips and kicked over the white pile of socks. "Yeah. He's so awkward, but I finally have a relationship with him."

"Tell him that. Tell him you want to keep up your relationship no matter what happens with him and your mom."

"What if she starts to come over with him too? She's going to drop the nice face the second he goes back to her."

"Girl, you know she's not coming over here when she gets him back."

Jess rubbed her forehead with the heel of her palm. "You're probably right."

Pam got up and gave Jess a long hug.

"Unrelated," she asked with her chin on Jess's shoulder. "Can I help you with the socks?"

"It's bothering the shit out of you, isn't it?"

"God, yes."

Pam was right. Two weeks later, John moved back home. He knocked on Jess's door every Thursday, but he always came alone.

10

On the first day of summer vacation, Kevin sat on an uncomfortable wrought iron chair outside Flynn's Bakery, writing in the remaining pages of his math notebook and sipping his café au lait. Though he preferred the comfort of the desk in his bedroom, writing at the bakery made him feel like a real writer. When he got older, he thought, he'd swap the sugary coffee for scotch and cigarettes, like old pictures he'd seen of novelists, typing away in a haze of smoke. Writing in his sixth-grade math notebook was even better. He'd only filled half of it with equations that he had never fully understood. Filling the rest of it with people and words felt like an act of rebellion. He wasn't sure if it was really rebellion if he was the only one who knew about it and the school year was over, but it made him feel good anyway.

"Hey Kevin," Toby said, his dog Pepper sniffing the sidewalk as they approached the bakery.

Pepper's tail wagged double-time when she noticed Kevin, pulling against the leash to get to him. She nudged Kevin's leg with her snout and licked his kneecap. Kevin scratched behind a long ear. "Hi, Pepper."

"What are you doing here so early?" Toby asked. He took the seat across from Kevin. "School's out. Shouldn't you be sleeping half the day?"

"I can't sleep late."

"I never could either. Maybe it's baker's genetics."

"Where's Aunt Amber?"

Toby smiled. "Sleeping late. What are you writing about?"

"A kid whose dad is an axe murderer, but he's the only one who knows."

"Oh. Wow. Not even his mom knows?"

"No. She should because she's a cop, but she doesn't. The dad is really good at hiding it."

"That's," Toby leaned back in his chair. "That's good, Kevin. Can I read it?"

Kevin hadn't had a grown-up read his stuff besides his mom. "Um. Let me work on it a little bit more."

"Okay. Maybe you can read me something when we're at the beach."

"Do you think the beach will be weird?"

"Yes," Toby answered without hesitation.

"Then why are you going?"

"Why are *you* going?"

"Mom's making me," Kevin said.

Toby's hands covered his heart as if wounded. "It's not to spend time with your uncle? You kids are the only reason I'm going. And your mom. And Pam, Aunt Vivienne, and Aunt Lou. Everyone but my own parents, basically."

Kevin smiled. "I'm glad you're going to be there. I don't really like Grandma. I don't like the way she talks to Mom."

"I don't like it either. We'll stick together, okay? Me, you, your sister, Aunt Amber, Aunt Lou, Aunt Vivienne. We'll have our own fun." He stood up. "I'm going to grab some breakfast. You want anything?"

"No. Hey. Can I ask you a question when you get back?"

"You can ask me right now if you want."

"It's okay. You can eat first."

"Can you watch this old girl for me?" He handed over Pepper's leash.

His uncle's few minutes in the bakery were enough to make Kevin doubt himself. Suddenly, he felt stupid and wished he hadn't brought anything up at all. Why did he have to be so serious all the time?

Toby reappeared with a mug of coffee and a muffin loaded with chocolate chips on top. "You're going to have to help me finish this. I couldn't pass it up, but I'm not sure my stomach can handle this much chocolate." He set down his mug and plate, and took a dog treat from his pocket. Pepper snatched the biscuit and ate it on top of Toby's foot. "So, what did you want to ask me?"

"Well, it's kind of stupid."

"I'm sure it's not."

"People tell me I'm too serious."

"Aunt Lou just asked me how my hammer's hanging. I welcome a serious question."

"Do you think I still would have been born if Mom had known she was gay before she met my dad?"

Toby's eyebrows shot up. "That's a big question. Well, she would have had to know a long, long time ago. She met your dad when she was a teenager."

"She could have known then. Some teenagers are gay."

"That's true. I know that she used to talk about wanting to have kids someday, so maybe she would have had you anyway."

"It wouldn't have been me, though. It would be some other kid from some other guy's sperm."

"You've really thought about this, haven't you?"

"Yeah. It's my existence."

"I could tell you that none of that matters, that what really matters is that you're here now. But I've had the same kind of thoughts. I probably wouldn't be alive if my grandma hadn't left the convent."

"I forgot that she was a nun," Kevin said.

"She was a nun for a long time. If she'd never quit, would my mother have been born? And if she hadn't, then would I be here? And Aunt Lou? If there'd been no Aunt Lou, there would be no bakery that we're sitting in front of. It would be something else. If I think about it too long, I'll drive myself crazy."

Kevin studied the brick of the building next to him, so seemingly permanent. "Why did your grandma stop being a nun?"

"I don't know. I always figured she just didn't want to be one anymore."

Kevin wanted to think that his great-grandmother had had some divine revelation in prayer, saying that she should leave the convent because she was destined to have children, ultimately leading to him.

"How are things going with your dad?" Toby asked. "Your mom said he's been spending more time with you."

"It's okay. We don't like a lot of the same things. I think he still wants me to like all the things he likes."

"Like what?"

"Football," Kevin said with disdain.

"Ah, yes. *That* bullshit."

Kevin laughed. Uncle and nephew talked about the aggravating expectation to be into sports from other guys.

They were well into their chat when Rebecca spotted them from across the street. She hurried across the road, spreading her arms wide, her purse dangling from one arm.

"Hello, my boys," she said, kissing each of them on the cheek. "What a nice surprise to see you both here. It's been a good morning of bumping into my favorite guys."

"Who else did you see?" Toby asked.

"I saw Alan at Walmart."

"Dad?" Kevin asked.

"Yeah. I told him about our beach trip, and he said he'd come along."

"He's coming with us to the beach?" Kevin said.

"Mom," Toby said. "You didn't."

"We were talking about the beach trip, and I told him how much we'd miss him. He's taken family vacations with us since he was a boy. He mentioned that Betsy had been asking him to come, so I said he should. He said he could come out to join us for one day. That's a long way to drive for a day trip, so I told him he can stay the night if he needs to. That'll be nice to have your father there, won't it?"

Before Kevin could make his mouth say something, Rebecca looked at her watch. "I wish I could stay and chat, but I've got to grab a coffee and run."

Rebecca dashed inside.

"What the hell just happened?" Toby asked Kevin.

As if in answer to his question, Jess roared from inside the bakery, "You *what*?"

The few customers seated inside the bakery stopped doing whatever it was they were doing and gave Jess their full attention.

"Mom," Jess said quietly, both hands planted on the counter to keep herself from strangling Rebecca. "This is Pam's first trip with the family. It's the first trip we've taken anywhere together."

"You said Alan is still part of the family."

Louanne stepped next to Jess. "What's going on?"

"Mom invited Alan to the beach."

Louanne's head whipped in Rebecca's direction. "What the fuck, Rebecca?"

"It's just for a day," Rebecca said.

"Oh, just for a day," Louanne replied. "That's different. Let me get you a list of my ex's. You can invite them too."

"I don't see what the problem is," Rebecca said. "He's come on family trips with us since you were teenagers."

"We were together then," Jess said.

"And Betsy wants him to come. Alan said that she's been begging him to go. Has she not asked you?"

"She has, and I told her no."

"How could you tell your own child that she can't see her father?" Rebecca asked.

"I didn't tell her she can't see him. She's been spending a lot more time with him lately."

"Well, I want Alan there. You don't get to be in a relationship for twenty years and then expect the rest of us to not want to see him anymore just because you don't want to."

Jess rubbed her face with the palm of her hand. "Okay, Mom, listen to me. Try to understand the exact words that I am saying. I am saying that I just don't want him to come on this particular trip. We just got divorced. Can we give it a minute?"

"Well, I already invited him," Rebecca said. "Are you going to tell Betsy that he's uninvited?"

Jess took a deep breath. "No."

Rebecca glanced at her watch. "I've got to run. Louanne, can I get my usual to go?"

Louanne pursed her lips. Jess, filled with anger and nervous energy, walked out from behind the counter and picked up a mug and plate from an empty table.

Rebecca shifted uneasily under Louanne's gaze. "What?" she asked, then glanced at her watch again. "Never mind, I have to go. See you all at the beach."

She waved goodbye with a flick of her wrist.

Jess set the mug on the plate and held them in one hand while wiping down the tabletop with the other. She stashed the towel in her apron and set the dishes in the bin by the coffee hutch. Then she began wiping down the display counter.

"I'm sorry she did that," Louanne told her.

Jess kept cleaning. "It's just for a day."

"Oh good," Louanne said, watching Jess scrub furiously at a stain. "You're not upset about it."

Jess stopped. "Of course, I'm upset about it."

"Tell Alan not to come, then."

"No," Jess said. "It'll be fine. What difference does it make what I want anyway? It's her anniversary. I just wish she understood."

"Me too," Louanne said. She leaned against the counter and shoved her hands inside her pockets. "There's so much that she doesn't know."

&❦ &❦ &❦

The sun was setting over the Gulf of Mexico when Jess turned the van onto the long oyster shell driveway of the rental house. She, her aunts, and her brother and sister-in-law had caravanned, and the constant stops for the adults, kids, and dog had turned a six-hour trip into ten. Her body tensed when she spotted her parents' Subaru parked underneath the house.

The place looked just like the ones that her mom and dad had rented when Jess was a kid. It was bright yellow and raised high off the ground, with steps leading to a wide porch in the back and another one in the front. It was situated in the middle of a long row of similar houses on the beach. As tense as her childhood trips were with her mother, Jess loved that she could walk down the front porch steps and hit the sand. It was days of no shoes and the sound of the waves day and night.

Betsy took off her seatbelt and leaned over Jess's shoulder. "Can we go to the beach before we go inside?"

"Yeah, let's do that," Alex said.

The kids had ridden the whole way in their bathing suits.

"Beach!" Kevin bellowed.

Then they all started chanting, "Beach, beach, beach!"

"Let's take them back home," Pam said.

"No!" they all yelled.

Jess was only mildly aware of the conversation inside the van. She watched the beach house become closer and felt her chest tighten. She couldn't remember why she had agreed to be there. To make her dad happy? As a sign of peace to her mom?

Pam laid a hand on her leg. "You okay?"

"Yeah," Jess said, hearing how hollow she sounded. She pulled the van to a stop and gave Pam a smile. "We're here."

The kids started chanting "beach" again.

"Not until you help us get everything out of the car," Pam said.

They groaned but filed out and took as much as they could carry with them.

Aunt Lou and Vivienne's truck pulled into the driveway a moment later. They grabbed their duffel bags from the truck bed and walked over to Jess. Vivienne wore bejeweled wide-framed sunglasses, and Aunt Lou wore a bright pink tank top that said "Day Drinkin."

"Has the queen descended yet?" Aunt Lou asked.

Before Jess could say no, Rebecca said, "Hello everyone."

Jess's mother and father walked down the porch steps dressed in all white like tennis players. Betsy ran to John, singing "Grandpa!" and hugged his leg.

Rebecca pushed her sunglasses up her forehead and peered at them. "Where are Toby and Amber?"

"They aren't far behind us," Jess said. "They had to stop a lot for the puppy."

Rebecca tsked. "I wish they hadn't brought that dog."

"Pepper is lovely," Betsy said.

Toby and Amber's car turned down the shell road and parked behind the van. Pepper jumped out of the passenger door, her leash jerking Amber out of the car. Amber laughed as Pepper sniffed furiously at the ground.

Amber found most things amusing, which Toby had once told Jess was his wife's greatest quality. She appreciated the wildly absurd and little silly things in equal measure. Amber had wide hips and an easy smile. She had alive brown eyes and a bright yellow pageboy haircut. Rebecca opened her arms wide to her daughter-in-law and called her sweetheart. As much as Jess liked Amber, she was always jealous of her perky femininity and how much it charmed Rebecca.

"I want to go into the water," Betsy said to John.

"Let's get your stuff picked up and I'll go with you," John said. "We shouldn't swim, though. This is the time that sharks feed."

"Really?" Kevin asked.

"Evening and dawn."

"There are sharks in there?" Betsy asked, a look of awe on her face.

"It's nothing to be afraid of," John assured her. "We'll be fine during the day."

Betsy took John's hand and they ascended the porch steps.

The house was spacious enough for the eleven of them. There were four bedrooms, each on a corner of the house, and each had sliding doors that led to the front or back porch. The sprawling living room was filled with natural light, and had an "L" shaped fold-out sectional facing the television. There were glass lamps filled with seashells on the end tables and copies of magazines like *The New Yorker* and *Atlantic*. Decorative starfish stuck to the walls. The living room and kitchen were separated by a long dining room table.

John and Rebecca had already set up in one of the rooms facing the road. "Away from the noise of the beach," Rebecca had said. Louanne and Vivienne chose the room that looked out to the road, and Toby and

Amber picked one that faced the beach. This left Jess and Pam with the other beachfront room.

"Perfect," Jess said. "That's exactly what I wanted. Kids, y'all can put your stuff in my room. You're sleeping in the living room."

"Cool," Kevin said, carrying his backpack into Jess's room.

Jess and Pam's room had two single beds, a long white dresser, carpet the color of sand, and a curtained sliding glass door that opened up to the back porch. The kids dropped their bags by the dresser and went out the glass door to join Pam and John, who were taking in the ocean view.

Rebecca followed Jess into the room, looking concerned.

"Your room has two beds," Rebecca said. She wasn't quite whispering, but talking low enough for only Jess to hear. "I thought you and the kids could sleep in one and Pam and Alex could sleep in the other."

Jess had a feeling like her stomach was a beehive, and her mom had just slapped it, angering everything inside.

"No. The kids have the living room and Pam and I sleep together."

"I don't think they would feel comfortable with that."

"They're comfortable enough with it at home."

"You sleep together while they're there?" Rebecca said, scandalized. "You're not married."

"Because we *can't* get married. Aunt Lou and Vivienne aren't married either. You gonna tell them to sleep apart?"

"They don't have children. I'm just trying to help you be a good mother."

"Thanks," Jess said.

Jess dropped her duffel bag in the middle of the floor and joined the others on the deck.

She put her arm around Pam's shoulder. They looked out at the Gulf, while John led the kids down the steps to the beach.

Pam took in a deep breath. Her hair was pulled back, the wind blowing the loose strands around her face.

"You're beautiful," Jess said.

Pam smiled. "I smell like car trip."

"I didn't say you smelled good. I just said you're pretty."

Pam shoved her. Then she took Jess's hands.

"You're shaking," Pam said.

"Mom suggested we sleep in separate beds."

Pam scowled. "Seriously? She's going to do this here?"

"She said because we're not married and because the kids would be uncomfortable."

"Oh, honey."

"What if she's right?" Jess asked.

Pam took both of Jess's hands. She pointed out to the beach where John and Betsy were building a sand castle and Alex and Kevin were running around with Pepper.

"Do they look uncomfortable?" Pam asked.

"Not at the moment."

"We're showing them what it's like to live genuinely, remember? So that they learn to love bravely when they get older."

Jess remembered and nodded. She didn't want her kids to grow up feeling the shame she felt.

"Now, come here," Pam said.

She guided Jess back into the bedroom. There was a small table between the two full-sized beds, with a lamp and digital alarm clock on top. Pam unplugged the electronics and lifted the table, carrying it over to the other side of the room. She stood on the outside of one of the beds.

"Help me push these together," she said.

With a mighty push, the beds met in the center of the room.

"What was that noise?" Rebecca asked, peeking in from the porch. "You can't move the furniture!"

"We'll put them back when we leave," Jess said.

Louanne appeared with a tall glass of something frozen in her hand. She grinned.

"Good idea. Vivienne and I should do that," she said. She poked Rebecca in the stomach with her glass. "Here, Sis, this one's for you."

"What is it?" Rebecca asked, taking a sip. Her lips puckered. "It's strong."

"My woman don't mess around when she's making pina coladas."

"It's all rum."

"Yes, ma'am. That'll put hair on your monkey." Louanne waved Jess and Pam towards her. "Come get you some."

That evening, John grilled hamburgers and hotdogs. The adults split up into teams and played Trivial Pursuit. Kevin, Alex, and Betsy played several games of Uno, with Pepper snoozing on Kevin's lap. Jess noticed her dad cast a glance around the room and smile. He took Rebecca's hand and kissed the back of it.

Rebecca grimaced. "What was that for?"

"Should I not do that?"

"You don't do things like that. What's going on with you?"

"This is what I wanted this weekend," he said. "All of us together. I was moved."

"Shucks, John Boy," Louanne said. "We love you too."

John stood with a groan. "I'm going to turn on the news."

"Dad, you're on vacation," Toby said.

"I just want to see what's happening," he said.

He settled into the rocking chair closest to the television and took aim with the remote.

"Your fifth anniversary is coming up soon," Rebecca said to Toby and Amber. "Any plans?"

Amber shrugged. "Dinner or something."

"We've been traveling so much, we thought it would be nice to have dinner at home," Toby said.

"Our seventeenth is next month," Vivienne said.

"We figure we'll hit Vegas for the big twenty," Louanne said.

"But," Rebecca said. "You're not married."

"Not legally, no," Louanne told her. "We had a little ceremony."

"It's the day I took her name," Vivienne said.

"You did?" Rebecca said.

"You knew that, Mom," Toby said. "Vivienne's a Flynn."

"Vivienne Flynn," Rebecca said. "A bit 'n' heavy, isn't it?"

"I think it's beautiful," Pam said.

"What are y'all gonna do when you tie the knot?" Louanne asked Jess and Pam. "You gonna go Duncan or Larkin?"

"Or hyphenate," Amber suggested.

Jess glanced at Pam. "I don't know."

Actually, they did. They'd talked about it a lot. They just didn't want the kids to know that.

"Well," Rebecca said, standing up to stretch. "It's getting late. I'm off to bed."

"You're quitting?" Toby said. "We haven't finished the game yet."

"We can finish tomorrow. Alan will be here. I call him for my team, your dad and I need his brains to catch up to you all."

They were quiet until Rebecca's door shut. Then Louanne said, "Both of you should just change your name to Flynn."

Jess smiled. They'd talked about that, too.

෫෩ ෫෩ ෫෩

The bakers woke up first. Jess, Louanne, and Vivienne met in the kitchen before the sun came up and brewed a pot of coffee. They took their mugs and snuck past the kids, who were all knocked out on the sofa bed. Jess slid the door open as quietly as she could, and they settled on the deck chairs, waiting for the sunrise.

Jess thought she should start a conversation, but the saltwater breeze kissed her face, and she took a deep breath instead. She watched the sky grow lighter over the water.

A shark fin cut through the waves near the shore. Her father had always warned her about sharks hunting in the morning, but she'd never seen one. He'd told her that their eyes rolled over white when they bit into their prey. It was hard for her to imagine, on such a peaceful morning, that something was violently dying while its killer's eyes were blind to its destruction.

After Louanne finished her coffee, she left Jess on the porch and went inside to bake cinnamon rolls. She tried to be quiet. She'd premixed all the dry ingredients at home, so that saved the sound of the whisk scraping against the metal bowl. But it was impossible to be totally quiet. She slid the pan of rolls into the oven and laid strips of bacon onto a hot pan. After a few minutes of sizzling, Kevin's head poked up from the back of the couch.

He ambled over in his striped pajama pants and T-shirt.

"Can I help?" he asked.

"Wanna make the frosting?" she asked.

He nodded.

"Go wash your hands. I'll make you coffee."

They finished up breakfast together. Kevin turned on the oven light to watch the rolls rise, and asked Louanne how it happened. Louanne explained the science of baking and the miracle that was bread. She wasn't sure if Kevin was interested in her enthusiastic response, but he didn't fall asleep while she explained things so she figured she hadn't bored him too much.

By the time everyone was awake, the bacon was crispy and the cinnamon rolls were frosted. After they had their fill, they hit the beach. Jess had to practically tackle Betsy to get sunscreen on her before she ran out the door.

The first half of the morning was just like the beach trips Jess remembered as a kid. Everyone did their own thing—playing in the water, reading on the beach, sculpting with sand, and going inside when one of them felt like it. Rebecca spent most of her time reading on the back deck, with John running around on the beach with the kids.

Betsy spotted Alan first. Around noon, as Jess sunned herself on a towel, Betsy yelled, "Daddy!" and ran towards the house. Alan lifted her up and set her on his hip. Rebecca, John, Toby, and Amber gathered around Alan, asking questions about his new life. His presence was a clash of realities for Jess. On the one hand, she felt the nostalgia of having Alan there. This was the boy who had been in all of their summer family vacation pictures for the last twenty years. On the other hand, he was the first person she'd had sex with on that same beach, across from Pam, the person that she was currently having sex with.

"Where's Cindy?" Toby asked him.

"She had plans today."

"That's too bad," Rebecca said. "Well, you drove all this way. You should stay with us tonight."

"I got a hotel not far from here."

"Can I stay with you, Daddy?" Betsy asked.

"Oh," he said. "Sure. If it's okay with your mom."

Betsy implored Jess with a look, arms wrapped loosely around Alan's neck. Jess felt like the trip she'd wanted was fragmenting. But then, Betsy would have her dad to herself without Cindy. That was a rare thing for her kids.

"Yeah, that's okay," Jess said.

Betsy jumped down from Alan's hip. "Come see the sandcastle me and Grandpa made."

"In a minute. I need to talk with your mom."

Jess and Alan walked away from the crowd, down the beach where the waves hit their feet. Alan took his shoes off and held them against his chest.

"I wanted to talk with you about something," he said. "I didn't want to say it in front of everybody."

"What is it?" Jess asked.

"I'm moving in with Cindy."

Jess arched an eyebrow. "Wow. That's great."

"Do you really think so?" he asked.

"Yeah," she said, genuinely feeling happy for him. "Don't you? I mean, you're the one doing it. I hope you think it's great."

"I do. She has a house. Apartment living isn't for me. I guess I'm just nervous."

"Why?"

"I've never lived with a woman besides you. I don't want to mess it up again."

"You didn't mess it up, Alan," Jess said. "You didn't do anything wrong."

"You sure about that?"

"Well, you were a dick for a little while after we separated."

"True."

"But not while we were together. You'll be fine." She thought of something. "Cindy's straight, right? She's never told you she thought she might be attracted to women?"

Alan laughed. "No, I made sure to ask her."

"Good."

"How do you think the kids will take it?"

"They like Cindy. I think they'll be okay with it."

He told the kids when they all went inside for lunch. Betsy, Kevin, and Alex sat in a line along the kitchen island, eating sandwiches with bits of sand on their fingers. Jess stood next to Alan, while the other adults milled about the condo.

"Cindy and I are moving in together," he announced.

"She's moving into your apartment?" Kevin asked.

"No," he said. "I'm going to live at her house. There's a room for you guys over there. It's much bigger than the one at my apartment."

"Is it the room with all the exercise stuff in it?" Kevin asked.

"Her house smells funny," Betsy said. "Can we change the way it smells?"

"Are you guys getting married?" Alex asked.

"Why are you always asking if people are getting married?" Kevin asked her.

"Eventually, *somebody* will," Alex said. "I want to go to a wedding."

"We're not getting married," Alan told her.

Rebecca walked into the kitchen to fill her glass from a box of wine.

"Is she Catholic?" Rebecca asked Alan.

Alan blinked, looking thrown from the question. "Yeah."

"Does she go to church?"

"No, but neither do I."

Rebecca sipped and set her glass on the island, staking her flag in the conversation. "Maybe instead of shacking up, you should start going to church together."

"Why would we do that?" Alan asked.

Rebecca's tone was nonchalant as she said, "I wouldn't think that the man who served as an altar boy for five years would ask me that."

"My parents made that decision for me back then. It wasn't mine."

"You can't get married in the church if you live together first," Rebecca said.

"Yes, he could, Mom," Jess said. "You know that."

"Well, they frown upon it."

"We don't plan to get married," Alan said.

"*She* does," Rebecca said. "She just hasn't talked to you about it yet."

Jess opened her mouth to disagree, and then closed it. Her eyes met Pam's, and they nodded in agreement with a realization that neither of them had to say out loud.

"Yeah, definitely," Jess said.

"Totally," Pam said.

Alan whipped his head from Rebecca to Pam and Jess. "Has Cindy said something to you?"

"I just know," Rebecca said.

"Come on. Cindy would have said something to me if marriage was on her mind."

Rebecca counted off her main points on her fingers. "She's in her thirties. She has no children, and she's never been married—she's thinking about it."

"That's sexist, Grandma," Kevin said.

"Yeah," Alex agreed. "Just because she's all those things doesn't mean she wants to get married."

"I'm not sexist. Where did you even get that idea?" Rebecca asked. "Your mother agrees with me."

"You're right, Kevin," Jess said. "Just because a grown woman has never been married and doesn't have kids doesn't mean she wants those things. But I think Cindy does."

"Why?" Alan asked.

"The way she looks at you," Pam said.

"And the way she is with the kids and your parents," Jess added. "She wants you for the long haul."

"You're handsome, single, and successful," Rebecca said. "What is she, a teacher?"

"She's an accountant."

"*I'm* the teacher," Pam said.

Rebecca narrowed her eyes, nodding to herself. "Cindy wanted to be a teacher but had to make better money because she was single. So, she became an accountant."

"Mom," Jess said. "You could just ask Cindy about herself."

"You're making assumptions too. You think she wants to marry Alan, but she hasn't said that to you."

"Yeah, but I'm not making up a backstory."

"Cindy has never mentioned abandoning a dream of being a teacher," Alan said, sounding tired.

"Why would she tell you about that?" Rebecca asked. "She hasn't even told you she wants to get married."

Alan smiled, his mouth tight. "It's good to be on vacation with you again, Rebecca."

Rebecca returned the joyless smile and topped off her glass.

After lunch, Alan changed into his swim trunks and joined the kids on the beach. Vivienne took charge of the blender, rendering fruity, potent concoctions. Rebecca kept her wine glass full.

Alan left with Betsy before dinner time. Rebecca tried to convince him to stay, but Alan said he would take Betsy out for pizza and he would have her back in the morning. Alan invited Kevin too, but Kevin said no. He was glad to have the time away from a seven-year-old, and he preferred the chips, sandwiches, and ice cream they were having at the beach house instead of pizza. Kevin and Alex took their ice cream onto the porch so they could scan the shoreline for sharks.

John filled his bowl with ice cream and clicked on the news. Amber, Toby, Louanne, Vivienne, Pam, and Jess sat at the table with Amber at the head shuffling a deck of cards.

"All right," Amber said, slurring from the number of Vivienne specials she'd had throughout the day. "It's time you all learned how to play Texas Hold'em."

"I know how to play Texas Hold'em," Toby said in an exasperated tone that told Jess he'd said it a lot.

"Me too," said Louanne.

"So do I," Pam said.

"Forget everything you think you know!" Amber said. "The Master will teach you now."

Amber launched into a ten-minute monologue of instructions. Jess, who stopped paying attention two minutes in, felt someone looking at her. Rebecca leaned over with her elbows on the island, staring at Jess. She didn't have an expression. That was the thing that really made Jess uneasy. Rebecca didn't look angry or sad. There was nothing but the unwavering gaze at her daughter. Jess mouthed, "What?" but Rebecca didn't acknowledge the question.

"Here we go," Amber said, sliding cards across the table to each player.

Rebecca stood up straight, wine in hand. She strode over to the table, staring down Jess. Jess's heartbeat shot up. She knew that look, the kind where Rebecca's eyes rolled over white before she bit down.

"You used to play cards with your grandmother," Rebecca said.

"Yeah," Jess said. "We used to play Gin Rummy."

"She knew about you."

"Knew what?" Jess asked, beginning to shake.

"When you were little, she said to look out for you because she thought you might be gay."

"I...didn't know that."

"Rebecca," Louanne said. "Where are you going with this?"

Rebecca shot her gaze at Louanne. "She said Jess reminded her of you. That's why."

"That's a compliment, Mom," Jess said, without the confidence she'd meant to put behind it.

"Want me to deal you in, Rebecca?" Amber asked.

"I told her she was wrong," Rebecca said, ignoring Amber. "I told her that there was nothing to worry about with you. It was Toby I was worried about. He was so prissy. But you. You had a good husband. You were a good mother."

Jess's anger flooded her body. She wanted to scream but just managed to stutter, "I'm still a good mother."

Rebecca tsked. "It's like you don't even think about the kids anymore when you make decisions."

Toby, Amber, Pam, Vivienne, and Louanne all started defending Jess at once.

"Rebecca. Jess," John called from the living room. "You might want to stop arguing and come see this."

Jess tuned out her dad. She felt so stupid trying to defend herself to Rebecca. To speak, she had to fight through the shame beneath her mom's stare and the anger that felt like a feral animal trying to burst out of her and scream.

"All I do is think about the kids," Jess said. "Before I make a single move, I think about them. You have no idea—"

"As a mother I do have some idea—"

"No," Jess said, shaking her head. "You don't. You are naturally the person who you think is good. You were born that way. I wasn't. I wanted to be, I tried to be, and it was killing me."

"Don't be hyperbolic."

"I'm not, Mom, I'm telling you," Jess checked that Kevin and Alex were still on the porch. She lowered her voice. "I was dying. My kids didn't need a dead mother. And the last thing I want to teach them is to lie about who they are and who they love because if I'd kept shoving that down I would have been dead or become hateful."

"She's right," Louanne said.

"Oh, shut up, Louanne," Rebecca said, "you never hid. You shoved it in our faces."

"I've seen it happen to other people. They die or become bitter. It's worse than anything I ever went through. There's so much pain and regret that they have over the years. And they pass all that pain onto their children."

"What are you talking about?" Rebecca asked.

"Jessica," John said. "I think you would all benefit from what's on the news."

"If I taught the kids to hide who they are because some people find it indecent, I would pass all my shame onto them," Jess said. "I won't do it."

"Are you saying *I* did that to you?" Rebecca asked her.

"Just like Momma did to us," Louanne said.

A crowd cheered. It happened so loudly and suddenly that Jess thought the commotion was coming from outside the house. But it was coming from inside, as John continued to turn up the television.

"Stop arguing and come look," he told them.

They all went to stand around him and looked at the screen. Crowds of people with rainbow flags were hugging and kissing each other, crying, jumping, laughing, and singing. The headline on the bottom of the screen said, "Breaking News: Supreme Court Rules Same-Sex Marriage Legal Nationwide." Pam gasped and clutched Jess's hand.

"Is this real?" Jess asked John, feeling shock more than anything else.

John nodded. "Court announced it this morning."

Jess squeezed Pam's hand back.

"This is disgusting," Rebecca spat and fled to her room.

Jess felt the sting of the comment for a moment but then noticed that her father was smiling. Everyone on the screen was rejoicing.

"Aunt Lou," Jess said, spinning around.

Louanne wasn't looking at the television. She was down on one knee before Vivienne, tears streaming down her face.

"Marry me," Louanne said. "Marry me for real."

11

It was 1:00 in the afternoon, and Jess was thankful that there were no customers in the bakery. There was prep work to do for the next day, but she decided to take advantage of the silence and pour herself a mug of coffee. She sipped, savoring the taste, and set her weight against the counter. Just four more hours until closing time.

Jess had been covering for Louanne and Vivienne for the past two weeks. They had gotten married at the courthouse on the day of their seventeenth anniversary and flown off to the Florida Keys to celebrate. Jess had tried to convince them to have a ceremony where everyone could be there, but they'd said no. "It's a honeymoon I always wanted," Vivienne had told her. "Not so much a wedding."

They were due back at work the next morning, relieving Jess for the first time in fifteen days.

She hadn't spoken to either of her parents since the beach trip. She had called her dad several times, and each time, he had told her that he was busy and would have to call back later. But he didn't.

Rebecca wasn't the parent that Jess wanted to see that day, but she showed up during Jess's quiet coffee time. Rebecca opened the door so slowly that the bell hardly rang. Her face was red and puffy. Uncharacteristically, she wore jeans and a blouse, the outfit she reserved for when she did the cleaning. A dull brown purse hung at her side. She glared, wide-eyed at Jess as she approached the counter.

Jess was so tired of that look. She tightened her grip around her mug and glared back. "Get out, Mom."

Rebecca's scowl slipped for a moment, as if taken aback. Then it returned, darker than before.

"Where is your dad?" she asked.

"He's not here. I don't want to talk to you."

"I don't want to talk to you either, but since you and he are in cahoots, I thought you might know where he is."

"Is Dad actually missing?"

"No," Rebecca said. "He left a note. He just didn't say where he was going. He said that I'll be hearing from his lawyer."

"Good," Jess said. "Now leave."

"You've lost all sense of decency, haven't you?"

"Do you mean since the last time you told me I was a selfish, disgusting person or just now?"

Rebecca's eyes bulged with fury. "Where is he?"

"Mother," Jess said. "I don't know."

"Like hell you don't," Rebecca said, pausing between each word so that Jess felt them land like jabs. "Do you mean that every time he's talked to you in the last few weeks, he never mentioned leaving me again?"

"No, Dad hasn't told me anything. And now I'm getting a little worried about where he is."

In fact, Jess felt betrayed that he hadn't said anything to her about it. They'd been getting so close.

Rebecca searched Jess's eyes, really looking at her now. The anger drained out of Rebecca's face. She laid her hands on the pastry case. "You really don't know."

"That's what I've been trying to tell you."

"Tell him to come back," Rebecca said. "He listens to you. If you tell him to come home, he will."

"He's a grown man. I'm not going to tell him what to do."

"You don't have to demand it. Ask him to. He'll respond better if it's a choice."

"I don't think he'll appreciate being manipulated anymore than being told what to do."

Rebecca's hands balled into fists. "You're just going to let him leave me?"

"Honestly, why wouldn't you want him to?" Jess asked.

"Why wouldn't I want him to *leave me*?"

"Do you love Dad?"

"Of course I do," Rebecca said indignantly.

"What do you love about him?"

"That's the kind of stupid question people ask when they don't understand marriage."

"I think it's easier for you to make me feel stupid than to answer the question."

Rebecca hitched up the strap of her purse and turned her body towards the door. "I don't know why I came in here to talk to you."

"Think about it," Jess said. Rebecca stopped. "You don't seem any happier with him than he is with you. I know you don't want to get divorced—nobody, by the way, wants to get divorced. I'm just asking you if you really love Dad or if you just don't want to be divorced."

Rebecca stared blankly at Jess. For a moment, it seemed like she was really considering the question. Then she said, "I just won't agree to one. If I don't agree to a divorce, we're still married."

Jess was almost impressed with Rebecca's ability to stay in denial. But mostly, she felt sorry for her, which was something she wasn't expecting to feel.

"Well, you're here. Do you want some coffee? I can make your usual."

The corner of Rebecca's mouth twitched, trying to smile. "No, I should go." She glanced behind Jess. "Where is Louanne?"

"She and Vivienne are on their honeymoon. They got married a couple of weeks ago."

Rebecca grimaced. "Okay. If you hear from your dad, just let me know he's okay."

Four hours later, Jess stepped outside and locked the bakery door. She noticed her reflection in the glass—hair in a disorganized bun, a dusting of flour on her temple, and her eyes half open with exhaustion. For a moment, she got an idea of what she would look like when she got old. From the crow's feet that stretched from the corners of her eyes, it wasn't hard to see how other lines would form in the hollows of her cheeks and the edges of her lips.

Her car was parked across the street, but she wasn't ready to go home yet. Once she walked through the door, the kids would pounce on her with questions and demands. What's for dinner? Where are we going tonight? I need a ride, and so on.

She passed her car and began to walk down the sidewalk with no destination in mind. She stared into shop windows without really seeing anything.

Eventually, she reached the wide cement steps that led to the great, old wooden doors of St. Mary's Church. She'd scurried up those steps hundreds of times as a child. Then later, she'd gathered the skirts of her wedding dress and climbed up the steps as a bride. A few years after that, she'd held the hands of her children and led them to the grand doors.

Taking those steps now, she tried to remember the last time she'd been there. She and Alan had gone every Sunday, unless one of them or the kids were sick. It was like trying to remember the last kiss before a breakup. She probably hadn't entered the church thinking that it would be the last time. All she could remember was a sense of not belonging, which she had felt since she was a child.

She pushed against the brass bar of the tall wooden door. The foyer floor was made of mosaic tiles, leading to a long aisle with pews on either side. To the left of the foyer was a shrine with rows of little red glass candle holders that shined like fiery rubies. The cathedral ceiling was high enough for Jess to stretch her head as far back as it could go to look up.

In the center of the foyer was a marble bowl on a pedestal filled with holy water. She dipped her fingers in the water and tapped her forehead, chest, left shoulder, and right shoulder. A drop slid down the bridge of her nose in a sloppy sign of the cross.

There were a few people kneeling in pews close to the altar, quietly praying with their hands folded. Jess chose a pew towards the back, not wanting to be too close to other people. She genuflected, pulled the kneeler down with her foot, and got down on her knees. She made another sign of the cross, and entwined her fingers on the pew in front of her.

As a person who constantly worried about things, she was surprised that her mind was blank. She had nothing to say to the God she used to bring all her worries to as a child. Instead, she took it all in—the high ceiling, the altar with the crucified Savior above it, the statue of His mother Mary off to the left, with fresh flowers all around her. The golden tabernacle, the smell of incense. How many generations of women in her family had knelt in that place, looking at the same statues, and the stained-glass windows depicting the Stations of the Cross? It was such a strange place for her to feel unwanted, since most of the décor was in tribute to the execution of someone who was also unwanted by the people around Him.

Her thoughts were interrupted by a voice who whispered, "Mind if I sit next to you?"

Her dad stood at the end of the pew, wearing jeans and a wrinkled polo T-shirt. If her mother had seen him, she would have insisted she iron his clothes before leaving the house.

Jess shuffled aside, making space for him. He genuflected and slid in next to her, stifling a groan as he bent to the kneeler.

"Surprised to see you here," he said.

"What are *you* doing here? Mom said you took off."

"I'm back at the apartment. I still had the lease."

"Did you keep it because you knew you were going to leave again?"

"No. I just couldn't break the lease."

Jess wasn't sure if he meant that he couldn't break it because of a clause in the contract, or if he just thought it would be bad form to do so.

"So, you're really divorcing her?" Jess asked.

John looked up at the altar. He gave a soft but firm, "Yes."

It was followed by a whimper of pain. He sat back carefully, relieving the pressure on his knees. Jess settled beside him.

"Why didn't you tell me?" she asked.

"I wasn't ready to talk about it yet." He took her hand. "Still not."

"Mom's worried about you," Jess said. "I told her I would let her know you're okay when I heard from you."

He nodded.

"I don't know why I came here," Jess said. "Do you think it's okay to be here when I'm not a practicing Catholic?"

"Probably not."

"I kind of miss it. Having God."

"You don't have to be without Him just because you're not Catholic."

"I don't really know who that is."

He nodded again, which frustrated her. This was the man who had raised her in that church. She wanted him to tell her who God was, and why, after trying so hard, she couldn't follow all of His rules and continue to live with herself. Then John closed his eyes and spoke.

"It's probably all simpler than we think," he said. "It's people who make it complicated."

"Then how do we know who God is and what He wants?"

John offered no answer.

ɞ ɞ ɞ

Jess tried to sleep in the next day, but she woke up at 3:00 AM, muscles tight with worry. Pam hadn't slept over, so with the bed to herself she stretched out in the dark, her legs and arms stretching to the four corners of the bed like da Vinci's Vitruvian Man. But in that drawing, the man's face was stoic, thinking nothing of his nakedness, unlike Jess, who felt so vulnerably human.

Her parents splitting up wasn't necessarily a bad thing, but she knew from experience that divorce was painful. It was like the death of something, and being the initiator of it had made her feel like a murderer. She didn't wish that kind of hurt on anyone, not even her mother.

Something else was bothering her, though. The first time her dad left her mom, it was bad, but this time it was worse. It seemed like everyone was moving on and leaving her mother behind. She didn't know why she cared so much. Her mom hadn't cared about her, or her misery. All her mom cared about was staying in a marriage to a man. Jess had been hoping, without realizing it, that Rebecca would change. That maybe she would have become the compassionate person that John had wanted her to be. That they all wanted her to be. Were they all just a family of people who all wanted each other to be somebody else?

Jess lay in bed thinking about it until she couldn't think anymore. She got up, brewed a pot of coffee, and switched on the television. She watched reruns of "Friends" with the sound turned low. It was a show she hadn't been into in the 90's, but it now had a comforting sense of nostalgia.

When the sun came up, she turned off the TV and changed into some old shorts and a T-shirt. She left a note on the refrigerator for the kids that said, "Gardening next door," though she was sure that Kevin and Betsy would be asleep for a couple of more hours. She grabbed her gardening gloves from the garage and went through Pam's side gate to the garden.

The garden had resurrected since the last freeze. There was lavender, jasmine, and begonias. Pam had started an edible garden next to the flowerbed—blackberries, tomatoes, arugula, banana peppers, mint, and basil.

Jess greeted the garden by tickling one of the birds of paradise flowers under its beak-like bloom. It had been a year since she'd planted it with Pam, and her life started to change. The thought of the milestone anniversary gave her a warmth inside, like the feeling she got when Pam kissed her.

Jess knelt down and pulled a few weeds from the base of the plant. The morning was muggy. After a few minutes of working, Jess wiped the sweat from her forehead and slapped at mosquitos. Pam's back door opened, and Jess leaned back on her heels, sweat dripping from her top lip, to see Pam step outside. Pam wore an open, green bathrobe and held a mug of coffee. She gave a wide, lion's yawn and bent down to kiss Jess. Then she wiped her mouth with the back of her hands.

"God, you're sweaty," Pam said.

"I thought that's how you liked me," Jess said, stretching towards Pam for another kiss.

Pam pushed her away. "Get out of here, you hot mess. I didn't expect to see you up so early."

"I couldn't sleep."

"Thinking about your parents?"

"Yeah."

Pam played with Jess's bangs, letting them tumble between her fingers.

"We have an anniversary coming up, don't we?" Jess asked. "Are we going by our first date or first kiss?"

Pam thought about it. "Kiss, I think."

"Me too. So, when is that?"

"You don't remember?"

"Um. No," Jess said cautiously.

"July 15th."

"Right!"

Pam laughed. "Don't act like you remember."

"I'm bad with dates," Jess whined. "You know what date I do remember though—June 6th."

"You want me to be impressed that you remember D-Day, but not that date of our first kiss?"

"No. June 6th is the day you moved next door to me. I know because Alan and I were going to the World War Two Museum. I was buckling Betsy's car seat and your moving van pulled up. Then this gorgeous woman stepped out of the driver's seat."

"I wish I remembered that. I must have been pretty focused on the house. It's the only place I've ever owned. But when I *did* notice you..."

Pam leaned down to give Jess a deep kiss. She tasted like sweet coffee. Then she stood up straight and stretched, mug held high. "I'm going to go change and join you."

She returned a little later with a long, open cardboard box of baby plants in black plastic pots.

"We're planting more?" Jess asked.

"Yes, ma'am," Pam said, setting the box of sprouts on the ground. She knelt down next to Jess. "I promised Betsy we'd plant strawberries today."

Over the next hour, the kids came into the yard one by one. Pam directed them to work various chores—Kevin was in charge of deadheading the flowers, Alex pulled up the tomato plants that had died and planted new ones, and Betsy dug little holes for the strawberry plants. Jess played her favorite Shins album, *Oh, Inverted World*, on her phone.

When the kids' faces started to redden, Jess told them to grab the sunscreen and their hats. Kevin came back with a baseball cap, and Betsy wore her tiara.

"That's not quite what I meant," Jess told her. "You need something that covers your head."

"But those hats are ugly," Betsy complained. "And I have to go all the way back in the house."

Kevin pointed next door. "It's right there, dummy."

"Why do we have to go back and forth all the time?" Betsy asked. "Why don't we just have one house?"

"We *could* make it all one house," Alex said, excitedly. "That would make it so much easier and our house would be huge."

"How would we do that?" Kevin asked.

He didn't seem against the idea. Just curious.

"We could make a tunnel that goes from my house to your house," Alex said. "But not an underground tunnel."

Betsy jumped up and down. "Like the hamster house at school!"

"The hamster house?" Jess asked.

"Yeah, the hamster has tunnels on his house, and they go all over the classroom so he can walk around."

"That would be so cool," Kevin said. "We could have a kids' house and a grown-up house."

"Yeeeees," Alex said. "Please, Mom, please, please, please."

"You're not getting your own house," Pam told Alex.

"But it makes sense," Alex said.

"But it doesn't," Pam replied.

"Hat," Jess demanded. "Go get it."

"And you two," Pam said to Kevin and Alex, "go get sunscreen. You didn't put any on."

"Are you trying to get rid of us?" Alex asked.

"Yes," Pam said. "Scoot."

When the kids were out of the yard, Pam pulled off a glove to wipe the sweat from her eyes. "We need a vacation."

"We just had one," Jess said.

"I mean, a relaxing vacation. Just you and me."

Jess thought about what it would have been like at the beach with just the two of them; sunning on the sand during the day and falling into bed together at night. The quiet and the joy.

"That would be wonderful," Jess said.

"I wish we could afford it."

"Me too. We do have a lot of extra stuff between the two of us. We could have a garage sale."

Pam thought it was a brilliant idea. They planned one for the next weekend, and spent the week gathering things to part with.

The process of it felt different to Jess than it had the summer before. At that time, she had been getting rid of things that made her feel like she was still married to Alan. Everything about it felt terrible then. It had been as if she was selling off parts of herself. This time, she was getting cash for a trip with her love.

However, Jess hadn't expected it would lead to her first real fight with Pam. They were in Pam's house arguing about whether or not to keep a painting of a bicycle leaning against the side of a café. Jess agreed that it was pretty, but, she said, what was the point of it?

"The point is that it's pretty," Pam said. "It makes the room feel relaxed."

"The room doesn't need to feel more relaxed. It's the bathroom," Jess said. "It's the most private, relaxing space in the house."

"That perspective is why you don't have personality on your walls."

Pam didn't say it in a mean way. She had said it like she was talking to a child who didn't understand art. Jess still felt cut. "My bathroom has a picture with personality."

It was of Kevin and Betsy in a public swimming pool, Kevin grinning with his front teeth missing and floaties on his scrawny arms next to a toddler Betsy in a yellow baby inner tube.

Pam gnawed on her bottom lip. "You don't think it's weird to have a picture of people in the bathroom?"

"They're not random people. They're Kevin and Betsy."

"Kevin and Betsy who smile at me while I pee."

"Has that always made you uncomfortable?" Jess asked.

"A little."

"They're not really looking at you."

"I know that. I just think that some rooms should have art rather than pictures of people."

Jess pointed at the bicycle painting. "That's not art. It's a random painting of a bike that you got at TJ Maxx or something."

Pam gave Jess the same look she gave Alex when she spilled nail polish on the kitchen table and didn't clean it up.

"I can't afford a lot of the pieces I want," she said. "You don't have *any* art. All you have are pictures."

"So?" Jess asked.

"So, if we ever move in together, I would want art in our house."

"Art's fine, but what's the point of having a mass-produced picture of nothing? Pictures of people are at least something that's connected to our lives."

Pam motioned towards the painting. "This is a reflection of me. It's my taste. All you have are reflections of other people."

"What's that supposed to mean?"

"I mean that you don't have any taste of your own."

Jess leaned a hand on the bathroom sink and jutted out her chin. "What?"

"I understand why you don't," Pam explained. "You've spent most of your life being what other people wanted you to be. So, you don't think about what you want your own space to look like, or what you even like."

Pam hit on something Jess had long suspected about herself but never talked about. She really hadn't known what she wanted her house to look like when Alan had moved out. When it was just her, the kids, and their stuff. She would sometimes see posters in stores or knickknacks that she liked, but they seemed random and disconnected from who she was. In her mind, those were things that other women bought and knew where to put.

"I just don't see the point in having stuff lying around that I'm not going to use or that's not sentimental."

"Their use is that they make the house look nice."

"Are you saying my house doesn't look nice?" Jess asked.

"Well..."

"So not only do I not have taste, or a personality, but you think my house is ugly?"

"I didn't say that, Jess."

"Yes, you did!"

The argument carried on throughout Pam's house. Jess pointed out the vase with fake flowers in the kitchen, the clay sculpture of "a blobby shape" on the bookshelf in the living room, and framed pictures of meadows and a Cathedral in the hallway.

"You're not even Catholic," Jess said about the Cathedral.

"It's beautiful," Pam argued.

"So are the Pope's robes, but I'm not going to hang a picture of him."

Pam crossed her arms, closed her eyes, and took a breath. "Why don't we stop for now?"

"And just sit with the idea that I don't have a personality?" Jess asked. "If that's true, why are you even attracted to me?"

"You do have a personality, baby," Pam said, softening. "I'm sorry. That wasn't what I meant."

"But you meant it when you said the thing about my pictures. I like them, but it's true, I don't know what else to put up. I've never been good at decorating. I don't know. Maybe it's just that I don't like art, and you do."

"Maybe," Pam said.

Jess fell onto the couch. "When we do move in together, maybe we should pick out stuff together."

Pam nodded, but didn't say anything.

"Are you nervous about what I would pick?" Jess asked.

Pam allowed a smile to creep across her face. "A little."

Jess blew out a puff of air. "Why do you even like me?"

Pam sat next to her and took her hand. "You've got a great ass."

They both started laughing.

"You said *when* we move in together," Pam pointed out.

"I did. Despite your terrible taste in art."

"I'm sorry I hurt your feelings. I didn't mean to."

"I know. It just hit on something I always wondered about myself."

"You do have a wonderful personality, Jess."

Jess kissed her and touched her forehead against Pam's. "And you've got a great ass."

᪣᪣᪣

The day of the yard sale was unseasonably cool for July. There were clouds, but no chance of rain. There was one rolling rack of clothes the kids had grown out of, and two more racks of clothes that Pam and Jess admitted they wouldn't fit into again. The folding tables were covered in toys the kids weren't interested in anymore, Pam's air fryer, a coffee machine, jewelry, and wall decor (including the bicycle painting). Nothing with "bride" or "groom" written on it.

Among the items for sale was Betsy's training-wheel bike with Princess Elsa on the seat. She'd gotten a new, red, big-girl bike, and Alex was teaching her how to ride on two wheels in the grass while Pam and Jess sat in lawn chairs waiting for people to stop by. Kevin was inside, working on a new play.

They'd had a good crowd the hour before, but no one was there at the moment. Lindsey jogged past, lifting a hand in greeting but not stopping.

She had recently told Jess that she was sorry they hadn't talked in a while. She was happy for Jess and Pam, but it was difficult for her and her husband to explain to their kids, who they were trying to raise Christian. "You understand," she'd said.

Mr. Howard rode by on his bike blaring "A Little Less Conversation" from the boombox in his basket.

Jess looked over Pam's shoulder as Pam scrolled through listings of cabins in the Blue Ridge Mountains on her phone. They would not be going to the beach this time.

A car pulled up and two ladies who looked to be about Jess's age stepped out to look through the clothes.

"You think they're together?" Jess whispered.

"You always think two women are together."

"Yeah, but look at them."

One woman held a sleeveless sundress in front of her while the other gazed critically. There was something about the look that, to Jess, seemed to say that she knew her friend's body.

"You're crazy," Pam said.

"Maybe, but that girl is thinking about how to get her friend out of that dress."

Pam laughed. "You're thinking that because you've gotten me out of it before."

"That's right. If that dress could talk."

Jess's phone rang. She saw the word "Mom" appear on her screen. She showed it to Pam.

"You don't have to answer," Pam told her.

Another couple of rings and it would go to voicemail. She imagined Rebecca leaving a message, begging Jess to tell her father to come back. Jess answered the phone.

"Hi," Rebecca said.

Betsy gave a sharp cry from the other side of the yard. She'd fallen from her bike and was on the grass, cradling her knee.

Pam put a hand on Jess's shoulder. "I'll go get her."

"I can hear you're busy," Rebecca said, "I just wanted you to know, for what it's worth, I do love him."

"Mom," Jess said.

"That's it. I don't want to talk."

Rebecca hung up.

A car parked alongside the road, and a man and a woman stepped out. They greeted Jess, and she gave them a blank stare, still holding the phone to her ear.

All the decisions Rebecca had made in her life—would she have gone back and done them differently now?

"Momma," Betsy cried.

Jess walked over and bent down to inspect the wound. "It's just a bruise, honey."

"Kiss it," Betsy said.

Jess gave the knee a small kiss. Betsy hiccupped a sob.

"You kiss it too," she said to Pam.

Pam kissed it three times in quick succession, making Betsy giggle.

"Back on the bike," Pam declared.

"I don't want to," Betsy whined.

"Gotta get back up if you're gonna learn," Pam said.

Betsy took Alex's hand and climbed back on the bike.

"I think the fall just scared her," Pam said to Jess.

Jess thought of the decision to divorce Alan and to go it alone, only to realize that she wasn't alone. The best decision she'd ever made was to love bravely.

"Pam," she said, taking both of Pam's hands. "Will you marry me?"

Pam's face went blank, and Jess had a moment of horror that Pam would say no. Then, a grin broke across Pam's face.

"Are you serious?" Pam asked.

"Yes," Jess said. "Yes, I'm serious."

"Yes," Pam said, tightening her fingers around Jess's.

"Yes, you'll marry me?" Jess asked.

"Yes, please, I'd like to marry you," Pam said, throwing her arms around Jess.

Alex let go of the bike, and Betsy fell over.

"Are you guys getting married?" Alex asked.

Betsy had started to whimper and then stopped. "Married?" she asked with a smile as big as Pam's.

Jess and Pam stood together in a side hug.

"Yeah," Jess said.

Alex and Betsy screamed with delight.

"We can have the hamster house!" Betsy said.

"Yes!" Alex yelled.

"No," Jess and Pam said.

"Kevin!" Alex cried, running into the house with Betsy at her heels. "They're getting married! We're going to have the hamster house."

The two women who had been perusing the dresses walked up to them. One of them said, "I don't know what the hamster house means, but congratulations. We just got married two weeks ago."

"Thanks," Pam said. "Congrats to you too."

The woman holding the dress slipped Jess a five. "I guess this goes towards the honeymoon."

Pam and Jess looked at each other.

"I think so," Jess said.

The straight couple bought the air fryer and congratulated them as well.

Kevin walked out the front door, loose-leaf paper in one hand and a pen in the other. Jess couldn't discern how he was feeling from his face.

"You guys are getting married?" he asked.

"Yes," Jess said.

He hugged Jess tight around the waist, paper and pen in hand.

"You okay?" Jess asked.

"Yeah. Just don't ever get divorced again."

Jess gave him a squeeze. "That's the plan, kid."

Part Three
One Year Later

12

It was 4:30 in the morning, and Jess was wide awake in the bakery kitchen. She dipped her hand into the flour tin and lightly sprinkled Pam's name onto the counter.

Louanne looked over her shoulder. "Cute."

"Shush, I'm excited."

"You got a week to go. Y'all picked married names yet?"

"We're still debating. I already changed my name once, and we're both concerned about having different last names from the kids."

"Do you think they'd care?"

The phone rang. Jess patted the flour off her hands with a dry rag and answered, "Flynn's Bakery."

"I hear you're getting married."

Jess's body reacted to her mother's voice as if she was in a car that came to a sudden stop.

She hadn't heard from Rebecca since the day of the garage sale the year before. She knew from her dad that Rebecca blamed Jess and Louanne for the divorce, as if they'd put an idea in John's head that she wasn't good enough for him. Without John to thaw her, Rebecca's tendency to freeze Jess out had resulted in a year of silence.

"Mom?" Jess asked.

"Oh good, you remember who I am. Toby says you're getting remarried. Well, are you or aren't you?"

Jess steeled herself. She tightened her grip around the receiver. "I am."

"Why am I not invited?"

"...This *is* my mom, right? Rebecca Duncan?"

"You know it's me," Rebecca snapped.

"Rebecca Flynn Duncan?"

"Jessica, it's your mother."

"It sounds like you, but your words don't make sense. You want to come to my wedding?"

"Of course I do," she said, sounding exasperated.

"You've never supported me and Pam."

"That doesn't mean I don't want to come to the wedding. It's insulting that your father got an invite but not me."

Jess sat on the stool by the phone. "You want to come because you weren't invited?"

"I should have been invited."

"So, if I had sent you an invitation, you wouldn't have wanted to come?"

"Don't mess with my head."

"This is the first time I've talked to you in a year. How am I confused in the first thirty seconds?" Jess asked.

"Am I invited to your wedding or not?"

Jess's mouth opened and closed like a gasping fish. Despite the time that had passed and the hurt and anger she still felt, she couldn't make herself say the word "no."

"Um," Jess said. "Yes?"

"Good. Send me the invite so that I can RSVP. I might still decline. I have golf that morning *to which I was invited.*"

"Nice," Jess thought to herself. "Okay, well, it was good catching up with you, Mom."

Jess was about to hang up when Rebecca said, "I suppose your father will be there."

"Yeah, he's coming."

"Is he bringing a date? Because I can bring one too. Miles Humphry has always been crazy about me."

"Miles Humphry?" Jess asked.

"From the Neighborhood Association."

"Mom, I have to get back to work."

"His apartment is much nicer than your father's."

"You've been to this guy's apartment?"

There was a silence. "For parties," she said.

"Mom, I really have to go."

"Send me the invitation. I'm still at the same address. 584 Plinthe—"

"I know the address! I grew up there."

"All right, you don't have to yell. I just wasn't sure you remembered."

Jess hung up the phone and slumped against the wall. Louanne was next to her, looking nearly as distraught as Jess.

"Why'd you say she could come?" Louanne asked.

"You heard everything?"

"Enough from your side to know Rebecca's going to torpedo your wedding day. Why didn't you tell her no?

"I don't know, Lou, she sucker-punched me. I was confused!"

"Shit."

"Now I feel guilty." Jess paced angrily. Then, spinning on her heels to face Louanne, she said, "What do I have to feel guilty for? She doesn't even want to be in the same room as me and Pam. I never imagined she'd want to come to our wedding."

"Why does she want to come now?"

"She's insulted because she wasn't invited."

Louanne sighed. "Ah, Rebecca."

"She wanted to know if Dad's bringing a date."

"Is he?"

"I don't know," Jess said.

"Can he?" Louanne asked. "Please?"

"I'll ask him if he can bring a man. Just to mess with Mom's head."

"If John goes with a man, I'll go with a man."

Kevin walked home from the library with his eyes on his feet, one hand gripping his shoulder strap, and dark brown bangs in his face. He was thinking about the Edgar Allen Poe anthology in his backpack and how he wished his whole life could be made up of days reading in a quiet library for hours on end. No weird looks from people at school, and no having to learn about anything he wasn't interested in.

Alex rode up next to him on her bike. Her bubble gum pink hair stood out under her black helmet. Her mom had let her color it at the beginning of the summer as long as she dyed it back to blonde before school started again. She was still trying to convince her to let her keep it that way.

"Hey, Nerd," she said.

Kevin smiled under his hair.

"You ready to pick out our dresses for this upcoming situation?" she asked.

"Just because you got me in a dress once doesn't mean I'll do it again."

A couple of days back, Alex had convinced him to put on one of her dresses and allow her to put makeup on him. It was a long, black cotton dress with spaghetti straps. He looked at himself in Alex's full-length mirror and had to admit he looked pretty good. He could have done without the lipstick, but he liked how she'd done his eyeliner and lashes.

As a reminder, Alex stopped riding to scroll through her phone and show him the picture.

"Damn, I'd make a good-looking girl."

"That's what you should wear."

"No, once was enough for me. And delete that picture."

"Never."

"You gonna bring your boyfriend to the wedding?" Kevin asked.

"He's not my boyfriend."

"You make out with him all the time."

"That doesn't make him my boyfriend, and we don't make out *all the time*."

"He's a cool guy. You don't want him to be your boyfriend?"

Alex, who he had once wanted to marry, had come to feel more like a sister than anything else.

That wasn't to say that Kevin wasn't interested in girls at all—he just didn't know how to talk to the ones who weren't his sisters.

"No," Alex said. "There are too many cute guys in our class. I don't want to be with just one. I still say you should wear a dress just to freak your dad out."

"It has been a while since I gave him a heart attack. I'll tell him I'm a socialist."

"You could be a non-binary socialist and give your grandma a heart attack."

"Grandma's not coming to the wedding."

That night, in the middle of dinner, Jess said, "Grandma's coming to the wedding."

Kevin dropped his taco. "My grandmother? Your mother?"

"The same," Jess confirmed.

"But why?" Alex asked.

Pam had rented out her house, and she and Alex moved into Jess's. Kevin and Betsy had surrendered the toy room that neither of them used anymore so that Alex could have her own bedroom. Jess and Pam had spent several weeks carefully transplanting their garden into Jess's yard. Most of the plants had survived, including their birds of paradise that seemed to be able to withstand anything, and they'd replaced the ones that didn't with new, vibrant flowers like fuchsia, foxtail lilies, and mandevilla.

Jess had kept the tradition of waiting until everyone got home so that they could all eat at the table together. They'd started later than usual that night since Betsy's soccer practice didn't end until after seven.

"She's jealous that I invited Grandpa and not her," Jess explained.

"Is that the only reason she's coming?" Betsy asked.

Betsy had stopped wearing princess things. She wore glasses and kept her brown, curly hair in a ponytail.

"She doesn't like to be left out," Jess explained.

"She cut us out," Kevin said.

Jess took a long sip of wine. "I get how you feel."

"Do you even want her there?" Alex asked, addressing both Jess and Pam.

"I don't, but she's not my mother," Pam said.

"She will be," Jess said.

"Does that mean she's going to be my grandma?" Alex asked.

"Oh God," Kevin said. "I'm so sorry."

"Can you just tell her not to come?" Betsy asked.

"I don't think it's that simple," Pam told her. "Your mom wants her to."

"No, I don't," said Jess.

"In a way, I think you might. Don't you?"

"I would want my mom to come to our wedding if she loved and supported us, not because she feels slighted. Now," she said, "eat up so we can find clothes for you all to wear."

Betsy groaned. "All you guys talk about is the wedding."

"It's two weeks away," Jess said.

"Thirteen days," Pam corrected.

Jess and Pam looked over their plates at each other and shared a shy smile.

"I'm not hungry," Betsy said. She pushed out her chair away from the table and left her plate.

"Can I have your tacos?" Alex called to her.

Betsy turned midstride, grabbed her plate, and took it with her into her room.

"Should I go talk to her or let her be?" Jess asked Pam.

"I'll go talk to her," said Kevin.

He crammed the last bite into his mouth and followed his sister.

Betsy's pink, sparkly things had come down from her walls and shelves. Rocks, geodes, posters of wild animals, and pictures of the American Women's Soccer League took their place. She had just started playing that summer.

Kevin plopped himself down on her bed. "What's up with you?"

"Nothing," Betsy said, sitting at her desk and setting down her plate.

"You don't want Mom and Pam to get married all of a sudden?"

"I don't know. I just thought, maybe, with enough time, Mom and Dad might get back together."

"Betsy, are you serious?" Kevin said. "Mom and Dad are terrible together."

"No, they're not. They don't fight anymore."

"They don't fight because they're not together. You were too little; you don't remember how much they fought. Mom and Pam, like, never fight. And Dad's happier now, too."

"Mom and Pam fight sometimes," Betsy said.

"Yeah, but it's different. It's nothing like Mom and Dad yelling."

"I don't remember the yelling," Betsy said. "It would all just be less weird if they were still married. We'd see Dad every day. Grandma wouldn't have cut us off."

"Mom and Pam aren't weird."

"They touch each other too much. It's gross. Mom and Dad weren't like that."

"That's because Mom's gay and Dad's a robot. I don't even know how they had us."

"They were too touchy at my game last weekend. Now, some of the girls on the team are making fun of me. One of them freaks out if I get too close to her, like I'm going to touch her."

"Those little bitches," Kevin said. "It's Mom who's gay, not you."

"They act like it is. What do you do when people make fun of you?"

"I try to pretend it doesn't bother me. It doesn't really work."

Betsy sighed. "I think I want to be by myself for a little while."

"Sure." Kevin stood up and stretched out his arms. "Do you need a hug? Want to bring it in?"

"No."

"Of course, you do."

Kevin jumped off the bed and bear-hugged Betsy. She squirmed and pushed at his arms.

"Get off of me, you idiot," she said.

Kevin jumped back. "Okay. Just know that I'm here for you. A light in the darkness."

"OUT!"

"A candle to light your way."

Betsy balled up a piece of paper and threw it at him. He ducked and ran out of the room singing, "I am the wind beneath your wings!"

ಶ ಶ ಶ

The wedding was in the backyard. A bower, covered in birds-of-paradise blooms, vines of star jasmine, and cascades of bougainvillea, stood at the foot of the garden. Fifty white folding chairs faced the bower, split by an aisle down the middle. It was late afternoon, so it was warm but not so hot that the brides would sweat off their makeup.

Half an hour before the ceremony, the yard began to fill with Pam's co-workers, a few neighbors, friends, and family. When they were making the guest list, Jess worried about fifty people fitting in the backyard. However, most of the guests had arrived and were not crowded in. Towards the back of the yard, the DJ played Django Reinhardt on his laptop. Next to him were white-clothed tables with a two-tiered wedding cake and silver chafing dishes.

Jess wore a simple slip of a dress. It was white, with yellow and blue flowers cascading down like they'd been poured over the material. Pam wore a silk ivory pantsuit with flowers tucked into her hair that matched the ones on Jess's dress. She chatted up guests with a glass of champagne in her hand. Gorgeous, Jess thought.

Toby and Amber arrived with Pepper. They had trained her well enough to be a calm wedding guest, though she did immediately pee next to one of the chairs. She wore a white tutu, accented with fake baby's breath.

Alan and Cindy were the first to comment on Jess's appearance.

"You look beautiful," Cindy told her, kissing her cheek.

Alan looked her over and gave her a smile of approval, which was tight and out of practice. Jess had wondered how she'd feel seeing him on a wedding day that wasn't for the two of them. This felt right, though, for him to be there as an old friend and not the groom.

"Speaking of beautiful," Jess said, taking Cindy's hand and beholding the rock on her finger.

Cindy giggled in shy delight. "It's so much bigger than I expected. He really surprised me."

"Have y'all set a date yet?"

"We were thinking January," Alan said. "Gives us time to argue about the particulars."

Kevin stepped up to his father. "Hey, Dad."

Kevin wore a black suit, a white button-down shirt, and a white cravat. His bangs were parted and fixed in place with hair spray. Alex had helped him apply eyeliner and drawn a full mustache under his nose.

At the sight of her future stepson, Cindy pursed her lips. She didn't seem to know what to say. Alan found his words pretty quickly.

"What the hell is this?" he asked.

"Mom said I could dress how I want. I'm Edgar Allen Poe."

"It's a wedding, not a costume party," Alan said.

"I think he looks handsome," Jess said.

"Thank you, Madam," Kevin said. "I feel handsome."

Alan let out an exasperated sigh. "Bar?" he asked Jess.

Jess pointed to a table lined with booze, and Alan, without another word, took Cindy's hand and ambled towards it.

"I think that went well," Kevin said.

"As well as it could have," Jess agreed. "Go find Aunt Lou and tell her we're going to start soon."

John came over and gave Jess a kiss on the cheek. "You are stunning, my dear."

"Thanks, Dad."

He did not, in fact, have a date. "Your mom messaged me that she's coming."

"Yeah."

"So, have you both been talking lately?"

"Uh," said Jess. "Not exactly."

"I'd like you two to be on good terms."

"Good terms," Jess mused. "I don't know what that would even look like."

"Jessica," Rebecca said, sliding up behind them. She looked her daughter up and down. "Hm. I was afraid you wouldn't choose an appropriate dress for a second wedding, but this one is nice."

"Thanks."

"And Pam looks...handsome? Is that what I should say?"

Jess answered her father instead of her mom. "This might be the best terms I get."

"What?" Rebecca asked.

"How are you, Rebecca?" John asked.

Rebecca stiffened. "Well, I'm here."

"I'm glad you are," John said.

"Where are the kids?"

"They're by the DJ table," Jess said.

Kevin, Alex, and Betsy were hovering around the DJ, checking out his playlist. It was the most animated Jess had seen Betsy in a while. Betsy had been grouchy up until the day of the wedding, but had softened when the day came.

"My Lord," Rebecca said. "They're enormous. Kevin is...formal."

Louanne was at the altar practicing her opening lines on Vivienne when she saw Rebecca standing next to Jess. She'd wrestled with the idea of telling Rebecca something ever since she'd called the bakery and invited herself to the wedding. After going back and forth about it, Louanne had decided that if Rebecca showed, she would tell her. She still didn't know if it was the right thing to do, but she knew that she was going to do it anyway. She gave Vivienne a kiss and approached her sister.

"Rebecca, can I talk to you for a minute?" Louanne said.

"We're going to start soon," Jess told her.

"Don't worry, kid, we won't be long."

"But we might miss the wedding," Rebecca said.

"We won't," Louanne said. "I'm officiating, so they can't do it without me. Come on."

"Aunt Lou, I swear I'll make one of the kids get officiated if you're not back in time," Jess said.

Louanne led Rebecca towards the side gate that took them into the front yard.

"Where are we going?"

"Let's take a little walk," Louanne said.

"A *walk*?" Rebecca asked.

"Just enough to be away from everybody. I wanted to talk to you about Momma."

"Why do you want to talk about her right now?"

Louanne stuffed her hands into her pockets and stepped into the street. There were no cars out, just a couple of kids riding their bikes. Rebecca kept up without taking her eyes off her older sister.

"We lost her twenty-one years ago," Louanne said. "In all that time, I've been keeping quiet about something that she asked me not to tell anybody."

"When was this?"

"It was that day I came to see her when you and I had that big fight because you wouldn't let me in."

"I'd rather not remember that," Rebecca said.

"The fight isn't what I wanted to tell you about," said Louanne. "It's what she told me."

"I doubt she told you anything I didn't already know."

"All right then, I guess I don't have to tell you."

Rebecca crossed her arms. "You might as well now."

"No, no," Louanne said. "You and Momma shared everything. There's no need for me to tell you something that you already know."

"For goodness sake, we're on this stupid walk. You might as well tell me."

Louanne took a breath. "All right."

෨෨෨

Doris kept calling for Louanne. That's what finally made Rebecca open the door to the rosary room and let Louanne in.

"Wait outside," Doris told Rebecca.

"Momma, no," Rebecca said. "You're confused."

Doris shot Rebecca a withering look. "You think I don't know what I'm about? Don't tell me what to do, young woman."

"I'll be right outside," Rebecca said.

Doris patted the thin bit of space on the bed beside her, inviting Louanne to sit. Louanne lowered herself gently next to her mother.

Louanne had expected the room to smell like urine and unwashed skin, the way her father's room had smelled when he lay dying. But Rebecca and the nurse had taken good care of Doris. It smelled like soap and the yellow roses that were in a crystal vase on the dresser across from them. The blinds were open. Light streamed in on Doris's tired face.

"There's a wooden rosary in that bedside table," Doris said. "Hand it to me."

Louanne opened the drawer, thinking she'd find a pile of rosaries to sift through. But there was only one, placed neatly in the center. The wooden beads were worn from decades of prayers, Doris holding each one in her thumb and forefinger to praise Mother Mary over and over again. The cross wasn't extravagant. No silver, not even the crucified Lord. Just the simple wooden cross with no execution.

Doris took it in her clawed fingers, feeling the beads. "The love of my life gave this to me a long time ago."

"Daddy gave you rosaries right from the start, huh? I guess that's how you woo a nun."

Doris's eyes moved from the rosary to Louanne without moving her head. "It wasn't your daddy."

"Ma'am?" Louanne said.

Doris closed her eyes. "Forgive me."

Louanne couldn't tell if her mother was asking for her forgiveness or Jesus's.

"Her name was Anne," Doris said. "Sister Anne. Both of us had gone into the Convent hoping it would change us. We didn't want to be...you know."

Louanne knew what she meant, but said nothing.

"The church was the only choice, really, if you leaned that way. Or get married and pretend, and I didn't want to do that at the time. I met Anne there. She was the kindest person I'd ever met in my life. We tried to fight it, and the more we resisted each other, the bigger the problem got. We were together in secret for ten years. Off and on, of course. We'd try to stay away from each other, but it was torture. I tried to convince her that we ought to run away, try to live a life somewhere. She couldn't take the guilt. I was the one who found her hanging in her room."

"Jesus," Louanne said.

"Don't take the Lord's name in vain," Doris scolded.

"What in hell difference does it make now?" Louanne collected herself and changed her tone. "What are you telling me, Momma?"

"You got this problem from me," Doris said. "I'm so sorry."

"Wait," Louanne said, trying to process the timeline in her head. It was the only part of Doris's story that she could get a foothold of in the moment. "When did you get together with Daddy?"

"After I left the Convent. I thought leaving the church was the only way I could set things right. I'd driven that sweet girl crazy. I swore I wouldn't do that to any other woman or myself ever again. I just made everyone else miserable anyway."

Louanne's years of anger with her mother, compassion for her, and shock at the confession all sat in her stomach making her queasy.

"I think," Doris said, "I might have made you miserable most of all. You reminded me so much of myself, but you had none of my shame. It angered me. Why was this little girl so uppity when so many of us had suffered with the rightful shame of it?"

"There was nothing to be ashamed of in the first place," Louanne said.

"You might be right. You know what keeps me from looking back at my whole life as a waste of time?"

Louanne shook her head.

"I am so proud of you," Doris said. "I used to think you were big-headed, but I was just jealous. You are living the life I wanted with Anne." She smiled. "She's your namesake. Her given name was Anne Louise."

Louanne whispered her own name, as if rechristened.

"I think she would have liked you."

"So, you don't think I should have married a man or joined the church?"

"Lord, no," Doris said. She let the rosary fall onto her lap and took Louanne's hand in both of hers. "I'm sorry I hurt you so bad."

Louanne wanted to say, "I forgive you," but it would have been a blanket statement with no meaning behind it. Doris's rejection of her had caused her years of pain. Louanne wanted to know more about Doris's life, the one she'd never talked about. And she wanted to say to Doris, "I love you," and tell her that she'd never stopped loving her, even in her mother's coldest moments. But she started to cry and the only word she could get out was, "Momma."

"I needed you to know," Doris said. "But please don't tell your sister. There's no reason."

"Can I tell Vivienne?"

Doris mused on that a moment. Then she nodded. "Tell her I'm sorry. But don't tell Rebecca and the kids. And keep an eye on Jessica. I worry about that one."

"I will."

"Promise me."

"I promise."

"And keep this," Doris said, holding out the rosary. "I'm afraid it will end up at Good Will."

Louanne accepted the relic of her mother's shame and love. She began to sob. With that object in her hand, it hit Louanne that her mother was really dying just as she was coming alive.

Doris patted her arm. "Come on, now. Brave girl."

ᔕ᙭ᔕ᙭ᔕ᙭

When Louanne finished the story, she stopped walking. They were standing in the middle of the street. She took the wooden rosary out of her pocket and held it out for Rebecca to see. Rebecca stepped back from it. "You're lying."

"Haven't you ever wondered why she didn't get married until she was forty? Think about how rare that was for women at that time."

"She was in a Convent for twenty years."

"A lot of gays went into the church to escape themselves back in the day."

"But she was married to Daddy," Rebecca said. "She loved him."

"She did. Just not in a romantic way."

"She loved God."

"She did," Louanne agreed.

"How do I know you're telling me the truth? You could have taken that rosary and made the whole thing up."

Louanne put the rosary back in her pocket. "You're right, I don't have any proof. You can either believe me or not."

"Why didn't you say something before?"

"I promised Momma on her deathbed I wouldn't."

"Why are you telling me now?"

"Because three generations of first-born daughters have been queer. Momma was born before 1920. She couldn't be out. My life was hell, but I had more freedom to be who I was. Now look at Jess. She's getting married by law. The only way she's able to do that is because people don't keep it a secret anymore like Momma did.

"I know you're worried about Jess and Pam raising the kids and if they're setting a good example. Jess loves her kids just like Momma loved us. But Momma was absolutely miserable."

"*You* made her miserable," Rebecca shot back. "You never listened to anything she said."

"She was sad, angry, and bitter in her soul, and you know it. That's what would have happened to Jess if she had stayed with Alan."

Rebecca fiddled with the pearls on the necklace. "Did Daddy know?"

"She didn't say. I wish I would have thought to ask her. Even if I'd been allowed to talk about it after she died, anyone I could have asked was dead."

"We should get back," Rebecca said.

"All right."

As they walked back to the house, Louanne figured that Rebecca was letting everything sink in so she didn't interrupt her.

"Do you think that John was miserable with me?" Rebecca asked.

"Funny. I thought you'd ask about Jess."

Rebecca continued as if Louanne hadn't said anything. "He's not gay...At least, he wasn't. Who knows. Maybe he'll come out tonight too. But he was unhappy."

"Have you asked him why he was unhappy?" Louanne asked.

"He said because I'm not nice."

"You're not nice to anyone who matters. You should probably apologize to Jess before you're on your deathbed. And to me while you're at it."

"Don't push it," Rebecca said. "Is everything you said really true?"

"It's what Momma told me," Louanne said.

"I read once that it might be genetic. I thought that was junk science."

Louanne laughed. "Well, whoever wrote that must have studied our family."

Things were coming together in the backyard. Guests were finding their seats, and the wedding party, minus Louanne, stood under the bower.

The afternoon light was honey-rich, and the air was sweet and floral. Alex stood at her mother's side and Kevin and Betsy stood next to Jess.

Louanne hurried to join the brides. Rebecca didn't know what to do with herself. There was an empty seat next to John. She straightened her back and went over to him.

"Is anyone sitting there?" she asked.

"No," he told her.

"Do you mind..."

"Not at all."

Rebecca watched his face carefully as she asked each question. He seemed utterly unphased, as if it didn't matter to him one way or another if she sat next to him.

"You're not afraid I'll talk to you or something?" she asked.

He gave her a hard look. She lowered herself into the chair.

"Are you not walking Jess up the aisle?"

John shrugged. "I gave her away once. I think she considers herself a free agent."

Rebecca crossed her hands on her lap. "That's disrespectful to you. And where's Pam's father?"

"He's over there." John pointed several chairs down.

"You've met him?"

"And his wife."

"Are they normal?"

"To quote our grandson, 'What's normal?'"

Rebecca sighed. "They've gotten to you too. How do you feel about all of this?"

John smiled. "Makes me think of our wedding day."

"In what way?"

"How happy we were."

"I suppose I made you unhappy every day after that."

"Not here, Rebecca, not now."

"Fine," she said. She folded her arms and crossed her legs. "My mother was gay."

"What?"

"Thank you all for coming," Jess said into the microphone. "If everyone is settled and comfy, we'll get started."

Jess passed the mic to Louanne. She took Pam's hands. "I just asked our wedding guests if they're comfy," she whispered.

"It was cute," Pam said.

Louanne asked if they were ready. They nodded.

"Good evening," she said. "It is more than an honor to be standing up here with the five most beautiful people I know. Tonight, Jess and Pam's lives and their families become one. If you know them, you know how devoted they are to each other, how good it feels just to be around the two of them, and how they treat everyone who walks into their home with love and respect. I've always been proud to be Jess's aunt, and now I can say that I'm proud to be Pam's aunt, too. To be part of their family and have the honor to be the one to marry them is a joy that I can't describe.

"As your officiator, not only do I get to guide you through this beautiful occasion, but it gives me the opportunity to give you a whole lot of advice that you can't interrupt."

She told them that what the old folks say about never going to bed angry was true. To talk, even when the last thing you want to do is talk to the other person. To spoil each other, be playful with each other, and support each other through everything. To love, love, love, love each other, and then to love each other some more. And to stand bravely by each other when people say that their love isn't real, their marriage is illegitimate, and all the other horrible things people think they need to say.

Pam said her vows first. She promised to be faithful, to be kind, patient, and to not stay up too late grading papers so that she's grouchy the next day.

There was a chuckle from the guests.

She promised to love Kevin and Betsy as if they were her own.

Jess promised Pam that she would love her, would try not to worry too much, and would play with her, garden with her, and be there for her when things got tough. She promised to love Alex as if she was her own.

Kevin handed Jess the ring. Alex gave her ring to Pam. They repeated words that Louanne told them. I, Jess, take you, Pam. I, Pam, take you, Jess.

There was dancing. Jess and Pam weren't big dancers, but they were so happy they didn't care what they looked like dancing in the crowd. Jess walked over to her mom and dad between songs. She kissed both of them on the cheeks.

"I'm so glad you're both here," she said.

"Congratulations," Rebecca said.

It was a generic word, void of any warmth, but the acknowledgement overcame Jess. She wrapped her arms around her mom.

"All right, okay, that's enough," Rebecca said, as Jess continued to squeeze.

"Thank you," Jess said.

Jess went over to Pam, who was hugging and kissing her own parents.

"That was good of you to say," John said.

"Well," Rebecca said. "Seems to be important to her."

"So," John said. "You were saying that Doris was—"

"According to Louanne, yes. I don't know why I told you that. Maybe it's because you're one of the few people in my life who knew her."

"Yeah. Wow. I guess it explains a lot."

"I'm going to go," Rebecca declared.

"Oh?"

"I did what I said I would. I came, I watched it. I got information that I need to process with wine."

"Rebecca," John said, catching her as she walked away. "If you need to talk, you can give me a call."

Rebecca smiled. "You said I'm too mean. Well, you're too nice."

Alex stood next to John, imitating his stance with her arms folded, watching Rebecca walk away.

Alex shook her head. "Another grandmother I'll only see once a year."

"You've got a new grandpa," John said.

"Heeeey, I do," she said. She clutched John's arm. "Kevin! Betsy! This guy's MY grandpa now!"

Kevin and Betsy emerged from the dancers.

"He's still our grandpa," Betsy said.

"She's our sister now," Kevin said.

Betsy lowered her face to hide a smile. "I have a sister."

"I've got two!" Kevin said.

Alex took off her heels, grabbed Kevin and Betsy's hands, and jumped up and down. "You're my brother and sister, you're my brother and sister, you're my brother and sister!"

John inched away from the ball of energy that was his grandchildren. Louanne and Vivienne hollered for him to join them.

They all danced, including Pepper, until the sun went down and the fairy lights came on, the ones that the kids had strung earlier that day.

"To the Mrs. Flynns!" Kevin said, raising a glass of ginger ale.

The remaining guests lifted their glasses, singing their well wishes to the Flynns, the name that Jess and Pam had settled on. Jess and Pam held each other in a sideways hug, thanking the ones who toasted them with happy, strange, beautiful lives.

Acknowledgments

There are so many people, places, and music that played a part in the creation of this book. First and foremost, my family – thank you to my wife Melanie, who rides my roller coaster of "Writing is amazing! I feel so feel alive!" and "I am the worst, most uncreative person who ever lived," and loves me anyway. Thank you so much to my children, Claire, Emma, and Christopher, who make me proud and make me laugh every day.

Thanks to my parents, Steve and Theresa Rheams, who have encouraged me since I first announced that I wanted to be a novelist in the 6th grade. Thanks and love to my sisters, April & Stephanie, along with the Rheams family – David, James, Patrick, Chris, Bill, Anne, and Beth. The Arceneaux family – Tommy, Barbara, Shirley, Paul, and Bethy. Cheers to my cousin, Danny, who cowrote my first book with me one summer when we were kids. Huge thanks to my fellow Bullshit Bandit and high school partner in crime, Jennifer Kurtz, who cowrote *The Daily Dominican Obituaries*. Thank you to my grandfathers, William G. Rheams, Sr. and Harold Arceneaux, who told stories so well that I wanted to be a grandpa when I grew up so that I could tell stories, too.

Enormous gratitude to the amazing Ian Henzel and St. Sukie de la Croix, owners of Rattling Good Yarns Press, who are "dedicated to the principle that LGBTQ+ voices need to be heard."

Big thanks to my work family in the Student Success Center and the English department at Loyola University, New Orleans.

This book and my brain would have been in a miserable state were it not for my writing partner, Morgan Hufstader, and the members of the Queer Writers of New Orleans and Third Lantern Lit.

Thank you to my readers who have given priceless, useful feedback and inspiration over the years: Thom Addington, Charly Borenstein-Reguira, Kathy Brock, Tricia Brown, Chris Cancienne, Suz Duren, Ed,

Beth F., Vicky Fraser, Alida Glass, Amanda Golob, Tom Harold, Barb Johnson, Bridget Johnston, Joanna Leake, Amy LeBlanc, Nick Mainieri, James Nolan, Thomas Peri, Desi Richter, Heather Sowers, Steve Sowers, Meri Spencer, Leigh Stewart, Ray T., Tina T., Kristen Templet, The Unholy Trinity (Steph, Adrienne, & Nikki), Dr. Arati Jambotkar Watson, Christy Wild, Fred Wild, and Alex Zemanovic.

To the places where I wrote the bulk of this book - Cork City, Ireland, and Zot'z Café in New Orleans – thanks for giving me a place to drink and make things up.

I'm thankful for the music of The Shins, The Brian Jonestown Massacre, Mazzy Star, David Bowie, Kurt Vile, Courtney Barnett, The Dandy Warhols, Elliot Smith, Fontaines D.C., and that one song "I Found" by Amber Run, all of which I listened to compulsively while Jess, Louanne, and Kevin played out scenes in my mind.

And finally, to all the brave LGBTQ+ humans who live and love authentically - thank you, thank you, thank you.

About the Author

Genevieve Rheams writes LGTBQ+ romance, comedy, literature, and personal essays. She received her MFA in Fiction from the University of New Orleans, teaches fiction writing workshops, and is an Academic Advisor at Loyola University. You can find her telling stories onstage at her local chapter of The Moth or Greetings, From Queer Mountain.

She delights in having conversations with her three adult children and going for absurdly long walks. She lives with her wife in her hometown of New Orleans with their two cats and a dog. As you read this, she is most likely out of coffee and litter.

For more information and stories you can find her at www.genevieverheams.com.